ON CUE

By Bettie Boswell

M ⳨ Zion Ridge Press LLC

To Mary,
Blessings!
Bettie Boswell

Mt Zion Ridge Press LLC
295 Gum Springs Rd, NW
Georgetown, TN 37366

https://www.mtzionridgepress.com

ISBN 13: 978-1-949564-89-1

Published in the United States of America
Publication Date: November 1, 2020

Editor-In-Chief: Michelle Levigne
Executive Editor: Tamera Lynn Kraft

Dedication:

On Cue is dedicated to my loving husband David and our family for supporting my writing adventures. A big shout-out to my wonderful critique partner, Ann Cavera: Thank you for your insight and helpful critiques! Thank you to Joy Brown-Latimer for always encouraging me in my endeavors. Without going through the process of creating a musical called *Just Around the Bend*, co-authored by Beth Jacobs, this story would have been less real. Thanks Beth. Thank you to Joy Armstrong, the Sylvania Heritage Museum, and the Lathrop House for historical inspiration. Thank you to all those who helped sharpen my writing skills through workshops at ACFW, SCBWI, Highlights Foundation, 12x12, Southern Christian Writers Conference, Ohio/Michigan Christian Writers Conferences, Seekerville, and many other writing groups. Thank you to Mt. Zion Ridge, Tamara, and Michelle, for taking a chance on this book. Huge thanks to my Lord for inspiration throughout the creation of this story.

Chapter 1

Ding!

The pungent smell of marinara sauce wafting from a splattered microwave filled the Forest Glen Elementary School teachers' lounge. Ginny Cline's phone chimed along with the microwave, leaving a discordant sound reverberating in her ears. Who could be sending a message this time of day? Most of her friends were the educators sitting around the battered wooden tables scattered throughout the warm teachers' lounge. She hoped Mom had not done something wacky again. She sent a quick petition heavenward, hoping the text brought the good news she'd been waiting to hear.

Ginny lowered her salad fork and shifted in her seat. She pulled her smart phone from her black dress pants and opened a message from Annie. The woman could talk a mile a minute and the lengthy text reflected her voice.

Contact me as soon as possible. I have good news. The situation has changed. We are going big. I need you to present your project to the museum board next week. There's no way I can do justice to it. They need to hear your voice. Do you think you could expand what you have now into an even longer event? By the way, I've invited some of our Northern Ohio government officials, too. We'll need lots of financial backers!

The words from the Forest Glen Historical Museum's curator sent a shiver up Ginny's spine. Did Annie think Ginny could expand the project on a whim? Saving the museum from financial ruin pulled at her heartstrings, but she preferred to work from behind the scenes with small groups of people. Convincing politicians to support her creation by presenting it through a written proposal was one thing. Giving a speech to large groups of adults meant singing an entirely different tune.

"Impossible." Her heart sank as she whispered the word, powered down her phone, and pushed it back into her pocket. She loved teaching her class of fourth graders, but she hadn't dared speak in public to an adult audience since nearly failing public speaking in college. When God gave out talents, speaking to a group of adults wasn't on her list.

Her attempts to minor in music floated right out the choir room door when she bumbled through her first solo during freshman juries. Her former college sweetheart did nothing to bolster her confidence when another disaster happened. She still struggled with the idea of forgiving James for embarrassing and betraying her with his actions. Thinking about the past made Ginny grit her teeth.

"Is something wrong?" Kara, her fellow fourth-grade teacher, laid a hand on Ginny's tense shoulders. "You look like you got some bad news. Did we get turned down for our fall reading class?"

Ginny relaxed the death grip on her fork and tapped a rhythm on the smooth tabletop. "No, we're in good shape for the after school reading program. The administration approved our paperwork and the library has space reserved on Wednesday afternoons. Sorry, I forgot to let you know." A sigh crossed her lips while she stabbed at her salad, which suddenly had all the appeal of wadded tissue paper strips.

Kara's brows peaked. "Then what's got you looking like your dog just swallowed a hornet's nest?" She paused as her mouth fell open. "Oh no, tell me she didn't."

Ginny laughed at the reference to her dog's voracious eating habits. "Jezebel is fine. I just got a message about an event that's taken up my time outside of school."

"Hey Ginny, what's this I hear about some secret project you've been working on?" Melody, the aptly named music teacher, joined their conversation. She sipped herbal tea and fingered a treble clef necklace as she tilted her head closer to hear her answer.

A quick glance at the clock gave Ginny the excuse she needed. "I've got to go. Come by my room after school and we'll talk about this later."

Twenty-five excited children would soon line up from their final recess. She capped her ginger ale and forced down one more bite of her tasteless salad.

"Have a relaxing summer, everyone."

Relaxing would not be on her summer list. If all went well, she would be busy perfecting her project. Maybe she could convince the politicians and board to read a letter instead of giving a speech.

She haphazardly stuffed her reusable salad container and fork into her zippered lunch sack and then darted out the door. She had just enough time to run by the office and pick up any last-minute mail before gathering her students.

As she dashed toward her destination, the empty hallway echoed the clicking cadence made by the heels of her beige dress shoes. Bare walls and stripped bulletin boards--prepared for the impending summer exodus of students--provided a perfect resonating chamber. Glancing at the hallway clock confirmed the need to make every second count to complete her office run. One more turn and...

Oomph!

What? Ginny gasped as she slammed into an unexpected barrier, not normally found around that corner. The blockade solidified into a fortress of muscular manhood. Strong arms held her in place while the salad container and fork freed themselves from the partially zipped lunch bag. Lettuce and kale flew down the hallway. Her hands pushed against a firm chest. Ginny stared into a tie, covered in drama masks, music notes, and, *oh no*, wilted lettuce. So much for speed. The only thing racing now was her heart. It didn't pay to break the rules about running in the hall. Or, maybe it did.

Her pulse went into overdrive as her eyes moved from the food-soaked tie to the ring-less hands wrapped around her forearms. She looked up and found a full reddish-gold beard adorning the man's face. Dark sunglasses hid his eyes. Long, sandy hair curled around his ears. A fresh minty scent emanated from warm bronzed skin. *Hmm. Nice.* Having those strong but gentle hands supporting her arms proved even nicer.

It had been a long time since she had literally let a man get close. Perhaps too long... Full lips grinned at Ginny. Tawny eyebrows rose in either interest or laughter.

Stunned, she could not move from shock, or was it something else? Heat trilled through her veins. Did she hear *Ode to Joy* ringing in her head?

Reality came surging back and she pulled away from the much too welcome embrace. Leading men were not in her plans for the day. Not today. Not ever. Not since James. She had mail to pick up and children to retrieve. She needed to get out of this situation.

Quick.

"I'm so sorry!" Their voices rang in unison as they both reached for items strewn across the hall.

"I guess this proves you shouldn't run in the hall." The man had the nerve to laugh when he held out the drippy salad bowl.

"Thanks for helping, sorry again for running into you," Ginny blurted, edging away until she bumped into a cool wall. Her hands shook as she grabbed the bowl he held out to her, and nearly spilled the remaining lettuce shreds again. *Please help me, Lord.* Stiffening her spine, she drew courage from her brief prayer and zipped the bowl back into her lunch container. "Sorry." She took another step down the hallway.

"Nice to meet you, Miss…"

"Excuse me, no time, I've got to go get my class."

Before I die of embarrassment or throw myself back into your delicious arms.

That couldn't happen. A man wasn't part of her plans and might never be. Besides, if she latched onto him again, she'd probably scare the poor guy, or herself, to death. She pushed away her errant thoughts as she turned her back on the handsome man and escaped toward the school office.

♥ ♥ ♥

Drama professor Scott Hallmark smiled and watched the fleeing figure fade from his view. She reminded him of *Alice in Wonderland's* white rabbit, the one who always ran late. However, her long brunette hair and shapely figure bore no other resemblance to the infamous hare. A lavender scent followed her as she swayed down the hallway. Bouncing off the petite woman and her nearly eaten rabbit food certainly provided a unique way to meet someone. He'd noticed the absence of a wedding ring when he returned the scattered utensils.

"Very interesting."

She turned briefly before entering the school office through the door marked *teachers only*. He hoped she hadn't heard his comment. He hadn't meant to say it out loud. At least he'd stifled the urge to whistle. His singing and whistling sometimes grated on people's nerves. His happy tunes had been the source of irritation for several aspiring actresses.

Irritation had not kept his new church friends from doing their best to set him up on a date. They would be impressed he'd finally noticed someone. Just because he couldn't take his eyes off the cute little teacher didn't mean he would do anything about it, though. He knew from firsthand experience that looks and first impressions could be misleading. When he did settle down, it would be with a strong Christian, not someone whose only asset happened to be great looks.

Right now, his looks were probably enough to scare anyone away. The beard and scruffy hair needed to go once he finished tonight's dinner theater at church. His role as a vagabond, seeking God in a homeless shelter, had been a fun challenge. He'd been shanghaied into the role his first week in town when church members discovered his acting experience. He'd had a month to take on the mangy persona.

An early morning eye appointment had resulted in slightly dilated eyes, necessitating the sunglasses that added to his rough appearance. He'd be lucky if the woman didn't report a dangerous intruder lurking in the hall. He tapped his shirt pocket and felt the visitor sticker still stuck there. Thank the Lord for that little item. At least security wouldn't be chasing him out of the building.

Who would have thought dropping off flyers for his summer theater camp would be so hazardous? He grimaced and drew a tissue from his jeans pocket. He swiped at the spicy dressing still soaking into his favorite tie. The aroma of oregano and garlic filled the air. Italian dressing! At least she had good taste. Better than the last bleu cheese-gnashing wanna-be actress who used him to scale the musical theater social ladder.

He hoped teaching at a small town college would be less dramatic than the diva-eat-diva world of professional stage acting. At least he would only be working with young divas this summer. If there were enough recruits. The camp was one way he hoped to impress his new employer, Freedom College. They'd almost missed getting the flyers out due to a printing error and a forgetful graduate assistant. He needed to make a good impression with the college and that little fluke hadn't helped.

He dropped the soiled tissue into a nearby trashcan and made his exit. Being involved with another woman was the last thing he needed right now. He should not be thinking about pulling another person into an unknown future. Why did his mind keep returning to her animated face and long brown hair? There were other things to worry about, like recruiting a camp full of kids at the last minute and making sure everything worked out with his rent-to-own contract. The money for that gem of a home required sticking to a tight budget, but so far it seemed worth every penny.

Until he completed his tenure track requirements at the college, life might be filled with scary and unexpected turns. Especially turns at intersecting hallways in the building he had just exited. Maybe dropping off the rest of the flyers at the library would be less eventful.

A ping drew his attention to a text message as he walked across the steaming blacktop parking lot toward his mini SUV. The icon for philanthropist Edmund Bradley wavered in front of his eyes as he held the phone in his shadow and swiped open the message.

I need your help with a possible project. Give me a call.

A sinking sensation rushed into his chest. Not another request from the drama camp's benefactor, Edmund Bradley. Had he sold his soul to the man?

♥ ♥ ♥

Fleeing into the office, Ginny thought she heard hearty laughter and the comment: "Very interesting." She forced herself to take a cleansing breath and leaned against the inside of the office door, trying to calm her thumping heart. In, out, one more breath ought to do the trick.

"Are you okay?" Denise, the school's secretary and right hand person for everyone, tapped her pink fingernails on a desk topped with stacks of manila folders. Not giving Ginny time to answer, she grinned and said in a smug voice, "You must have run into that cute guy from Freedom College. He left some papers about a summer theater camp in everyone's box. Make sure you send them home with all your children."

Ginny stared in confusion as laughter bubbled from the secretary's mouth. With a knowing look, Denise pointed at the security monitor screens. Images glared, showing the nearly vacant hallway and front door where the man stood brushing a tissue over his tie. Ginny gaped and then snapped her mouth closed. This was not how she hoped her last school day before summer would go. Denise could be a sweetheart, but willingly gossiped when something interesting happened. *Interesting* didn't cover this situation. *Total disaster* was a better term, but Ginny didn't have time to dwell on the storm swirling through her mind.

She grabbed her mail and the camp fliers. She flapped them across her face, to cool the sudden burst of heat soaring through her body. Denise's chuckles followed her as she marched away from the office. At least her warm cheeks would match those of her students as they returned from playing in the mid-day sun. She prayed the afternoon ice cream she bought for her beloved students would cool them all down. Maybe she would have some to chill her runaway emotions. Many of her students only got treats at school and she loved going the extra mile to provide something nice on special occasions. She needed to focus on them for the next few hours and make their last fourth-grade day memorable.

❤ ❤ ❤

Memories of her collision followed her through the rest of the day. Supervising desk cleanups and going through lost-and-found items proved somewhat distracting. However, the occasional remembrance of warm hands on her arms brought another rush of warmth to her cheeks.

"You look kind of funny, Miss Cline. Are you getting sick?" Tina's sticky ice cream fingers reached out and touched Ginny's heated cheeks.

"No, just feeling a little warm from — ah — all the excitement of our final school day." Not a great cover, but it would do. Ginny pasted on her caring teacher face and handed a moist wipe to her messy student. She took another and brushed that cool tissue across her own warm chocolate-covered cheeks, before turning to the next chore.

"Everyone put this drama flyer in your backpack. It is about a camp opportunity during the summer." Passing out the papers for the theater camp experience drew her wayward thoughts back to the bearded man. His picture, with a groomed beard and lacking the dark glasses, smiled up from each leaflet. A cartoon balloon drawn near his mouth proclaimed, "This is your summer to become a star."

"Do you think he could make a star out of me?" Susanne twirled around and took a deep bow. The ruffles on her top fluttered as she took a dramatic stand near a box fan, beside the teacher's desk.

"I think you are all stars in my book." Ginny smiled at the classroom full of shining fourth-grade faces. "I hope everyone has a wonderful summer. You've been one of my favorite classes."

Joyous cheers rang out as the school bell buzzed one last time. Chairs scraped against the floor and then clunked onto desktops as students waved farewell.

"Good-bye, Miss Cline, I'll miss you." A freckle-faced boy fist-bumped his teacher.

"Thank you for being such a great teacher this year." Susanne hugged Ginny and then danced out of the room.

"Hey Miss Cline, can you tell the fifth-grade teachers to plan some fun field trips for next year? Your trips were the greatest." Derrick, Ginny's most outgoing student, gave her an enthusiastic high five as he sprinted out the door, not waiting for an answer in his hurry to catch up with one of his best friends.

"Walk!" Ginny's voice faded as he passed out of view and she turned to say farewell to other waiting students.

Melissa lingered near the door and brightened when Ginny wrapped her arms around the timid child.

"I'll see you next year, Melissa. I know you'll have a nice summer with the Russell family." Ginny smiled at the brown-cheeked girl who now lived with a caring foster family. Their Christian home would be a safe place for the hurting child. She'd only known Melissa for a short time. Knowing she would remain in her class for the upcoming year thrilled Ginny. Repeating the class would allow the youngster a chance to catch up on her studies, which had suffered due to neglect in a tough home situation. Melissa's carefully braided hair, ending in purple beads, gave testimony to the loving care she now experienced.

Other hugs, high fives, and happy wishes for a great summer flooded the room and then decrescendo-ed into a quiet hush. This class had blessed her by being one of the best groups in her five years of teaching. Their cooperation gifted Ginny many precious hours. Evening hours, typically spent working through student issues, had been freed up this year, allowing time to devote to her secret project. Funds raised from the event would provide another year of financial support for Forest Glen's Historical Museum.

However, now that dream would also require her to gather her courage and convince the board and local politicians to support their efforts. She just had to show the world she knew what she was doing. She needed the Lord's help because it would not be easy. Especially after Annie's lunchtime text--which she had failed to answer. Could there be any other way to gain support for the project that would save the museum? Only Ginny's shaking knees, prayer, and time, would tell.

Chapter 2

Returning Annie's call would have to wait. Ginny pulled a "School's Out" tee-shirt over her pink blouse, and hurried to meet the other teachers in front of the school for the traditional farewell. She grabbed an orange pom-pom from a curbside box and joined the frenzied line of teachers. Her voice chorused with the rest of the faculty as they cheered and waved wildly to their favorite and not-so-favorite students.

Children called out to their teachers with both joy and tears as the lumbering yellow buses rolled away from the school. Derrick waved from a backseat window as the last bus turned the corner. When the line of parent cars followed the buses from the parking lot, Melissa's face peered out the Russells' sedan window. Ginny raised her hand in greeting to the lonely child, then turned and gave Kara a warm hug.

"Have a great summer, Ginny." Kara squeezed her back and then bent to pick up a crumpled paper that had flown from the departing busses. "Hey, what's this I hear about you throwing yourself at some guy? Maybe you found your prince charming after all."

Heat rushed out of the stuffy building as Kara held the hallway door open for them to enter. Ginny hoped the warmth blasting from her face emanated from the brick building, not from an emotional response she planned on ignoring. She couldn't believe her grade-level partner and longtime friend teased her about bumping into the hallway guy.

"It's about time you met someone, even if you had to do it by running him down in the hall." Melody edged closer to the two friends and added her lyrical voice to the conversation. Her expressive eyebrows lifted as she looked at Ginny's face.

Ginny shook her head in mild disgust. News traveled at a fast tempo down the Forest Glen Elementary gossip line. Next time, she would swear Denise to secrecy. "Hey, I don't even know his name, so don't get your hopes up. Let's forget about him and have a nice summer break."

"Yeah! We made it through another year." Kara's comment rang loudly through the crowd of teachers heading back to their rooms. Cheers erupted one more time. Ginny's shoulders relaxed as conversations returned to final reports and summer trips.

"See you all in the fall." The principal's wish brought smiles to the teachers' faces. Budget cuts had resulted in lost positions the year before. It was a relief to know everyone would be back when school resumed.

Ginny shared a few more hugs and high fives with other teachers on her way back to her room. A stray flier from the drama camp lay on the hallway floor. As she bent to pick it up, her thoughts returned to the mysterious drama professor. She shook her head; there were better things to think about than some stranger wandering around Forest Glen Elementary. As she entered her classroom, she tossed the paper into the trashcan, and headed for her desk.

She sank into her chair and closed her eyes as she absorbed the peace and quiet that filled the room. Teaching was such a rewarding career, but she always welcomed the arrival of summer break. Sweat trickled down her face as she reached for a paper to fan her neck. Maybe someday the school system would spring for air conditioning. Ginny loosened the hair clip at the base of her neck and gave her long brown hair a quick swipe with the brush from her middle drawer. She pushed her humidity-induced curls into a high ponytail.

A tap echoed across the room as Melody and Kara knocked at her door and then entered. So much for peace and quiet...

"Hey, girlfriend, enlighten us about your secret project." Melody's voice sang with curiosity.

"I can't." Ginny clamped her mouth shut. She'd hoped she could drum up enough courage to at least answer Annie's text, but then there was that terrible word, *fear*. Like the fear filtering through her mind as she fumbled for an answer to Melody's innocent question. She could talk to her friends about teaching, but this wasn't something she had the freedom or desire to discuss outside of the museum's doors. Yet.

Melody was nice enough, but Ginny didn't feel ready to let a professional musician have the chance to laugh if her project failed.

It would not be the first time Melody had seen one of Ginny's musical failures, but for the sake of the museum, she prayed for success. So many things needed to fall into place before anyone could know the details she and Annie had discussed.

"Maybe it's not a secret project. Perhaps she actually found a guy. One who didn't run her down in the hallway?" Kara grinned as she winked at the other women.

Ginny playfully glared at her fellow teachers. "Only a leading man will do for me, and I haven't found him yet." Her last attempt at dating had proven leading men only existed in dreams. Ten-year-old fourth graders, who loved to play soccer and read stories about adventurers, were the only young men she planned to focus on.

"So if you haven't found a dream date, then what project is taking up all your extra time?" Determination and curiosity lit Melody's face as she leaned against Ginny's desk and wagged a finger in the air.

Ginny hesitated, then mustered a weak smile. "It will be something historic."

"*Historic* would be you finally going out on a date again. You've practically isolated yourself socially since college," Kara teased. The caring look she offered took the sting from her words.

However, Ginny cringed as she picked up a stack of papers and moved them from one side of her desk to the other. When she looked up, she saw compassion in her friends' eyes and laid open hands on her desk. Kara and Melody knew about the tragedy with James, from their college years as roommates. Back then, they'd been known as the three chickadees, friends for life.

"Listen you two, I'd love to share more information about the project, but I have to clear it with the Historical Museum first. Once I get the okay from Annie, you will be the first to know."

"Could you at least give us a little hint?" Kara crossed her arms and pretended to pout.

"If everything comes together, I'm finally going to do something with my musical dream," Ginny said.

"Good for you, girlfriend. It's about time you shared your talents. Just don't hide behind anyone like James." Melody put fisted hands on her hips.

Kara nodded. "Speaking of James, I thought I saw someone

who looked like him coming out of the medical complex last week."

"Please, don't mention that man's name again. I know I need to forgive him, but when I think about what happened, I can't. I knew better than to trust a man with anything so precious." Ginny paced to the door and motioned for her friends to exit. "I've got some paperwork to finish, ladies."

"Not every man is like James, or your father, for that matter. I think God has someone very special out there, waiting for you." Kara hugged her as she made her way into the hall. A hint of strawberry shampoo clung to her friend's hair and lightened Ginny's mood.

"Let me know if there's anything I can do to help." Melody paused on her way out. "This is your time to shine and I hope you have success with your project."

"Thanks, chickadees."

As she returned to her desk, Ginny forced her thoughts to the paperwork at hand. She carefully checked each report card for accuracy and tucked them into school envelopes. Then she placed copies of grades in files she would take to the office for next year's teachers. That meant facing nosy Denise again. The secretary had a good heart, but her lips were a little loose today.

Pride filled her as she remembered each of the children and their accomplishments over the course of the past year. Maybe some of her students would be involved in her project. Derrick should be a great addition with his outgoing personality and dramatic tendencies. Susanne's flair for overacting might be useful if she focused on directions. Sweet Melissa could benefit from participating in the program. The camp might help the girl get over her shyness. She sighed. The poor child wasn't the only one who had a problem speaking up around adults.

Ginny shuddered as she thought about her fears concerning speaking to Annie's group of officials about the project. A project that might not take place if she didn't return that phone call... *Give me strength, Lord. I would never even consider doing this on my own, so I could use a little help.*

She powered up her cell phone and waited for any notifications to appear. Sure enough, another message pinged with Annie's smiling moniker. The Forest Glen Historical Museum seal surrounded the enthusiastic curator's face.

We need to talk. Why didn't you call back yet? Stop by the museum tonight. I have more exciting news.

Tapping out a reply, Ginny drew on courage she did not want to have right now. But, she knew Annie and the Lord expected her to follow through. Saving the museum and making up for her past failures would be worth it--she hoped.

Sorry I didn't return call. Not real thrilled about being the presenter. Will they consider a written proposal instead? What's your other news?

She hoped they only needed to chat about next week's proposal to the board, not some other problem. Annie was usually more forthcoming.

Whatever she wanted to share could not be any worse than the mid-day text message. Ginny had planned on Annie presenting the project. Now it sounded like Annie expected her to make that presentation. She did not want to think about standing in front of a bunch of dignitaries. She loved teaching students, but the thought of speaking and possibly singing in front of adults sent a tremolo down her spine. There wasn't much choice if she wanted success for the musical and for the museum's financial future. She needed to remember the verse that said, "Be strong and be of good courage." Time to seek the Lord and not worry until the meeting with Annie...

After a prayer, she pushed her worries aside and concentrated on getting her final set of reports to the office. Denise gave her a smiling nod when Ginny breezed through the office and quickly placed her files in the fifth-grade cabinet. Her mind wandered as she inserted Melissa's lone file back into the fourth-grade drawer.

Help me show God's love to this sweet child next year. She has so much to overcome--another victim of a neglectful father.

Back in her room, she started packing up her collection of basset hound figurines. Her students knew she loved the droopy breed of dog and her collection grew each year with their thoughtful gifts. Sad-eyed dog statues covered a shelf that ran along the wall behind her desk. She wrapped the little replicas of her favorite slobbery hound in bubble wrap and nestled them in a corner of one of her locking cabinets.

Her mind rolled with regrets as she picked up an orange and white spotted hound. James gave her the little hound when they dated in college. If the dog statue hadn't been the spitting image of a childhood memory, she would have trashed it long ago. But, her love of the breed was stronger than the lack of affection she now held for the man. A man whose logic was incomprehensible when it came to relationships and betraying anyone who placed their trust in him...

His self-serving motives had ruined her dreams back in college. Too bad he discovered her weakness for basset hounds. She stuffed the little hound into the cabinet and pushed a box of science equipment and math manipulatives in front of the harmless statue. She should really get rid of it, but the coloring reminded her too much of her grandma's dog, Olive, and the summers they spent together. She slammed the cabinet door and shoved her key into the lock before turning to scan the room one more time.

She tossed a few stray papers into her recycling bin as she cleaned out student mailboxes near the door. On a whim, she retrieved a forgotten flyer with the professor's captivating image and dropped it into her bag to take home. Too bad the guy's name wasn't on the flyer. It only provided a secretary's contact information for potential campers. She hoped his name wasn't James. She needed a distraction from the past.

She tried to tell herself she only took the folder to share with Melissa's foster parents. The girl needed something to pull her from the protective shell she hid behind. Maybe some fun dramatics would brighten her up a little. Of course, Ginny wouldn't mind taking one last look at the professor's face. She chuckled as she recalled the way his mouth fell open when she bounced off him in the hall.

Ginny shouldered her bag and headed for the door. Any other cleaning or packing could wait for another day. Jezebel would be anxiously waiting at home, thumping her tail and pounding on the laundry room door with her paws.

Ginny's real-life basset hound, Jezebel, bore the name of the wicked biblical queen because she had destroyed many things in her puppy days and continued to devour all manner of vile objects since her adoption. Owning, or should she say being owned by the black and sable-spotted dog, had given Ginny an incentive to purchase a small house with a fenced backyard. Even with that, she found it best to keep Jezebel quarantined in the laundry room during the day and accompany her on walks outside. Before Ginny wised up, she spent oodles of money on vet bills and grew tired of hearing the veterinarian ask, "Now, what did your dog swallow this time?"

Fifteen minutes later, Ginny pulled into her short driveway. She heard welcoming bays resounding from the house. Popping out of her blue sedan, she walked to her porch and opened the front door to the white and yellow 1940s bungalow. She set her book bag next to the antique corner table in the entranceway. Sitting down on the seat of her late grandmother's oak hall tree, Ginny took off her dress shoes, slid on her tennis shoes, and then made her way into Jezebel's laundry room lair. After a slobbery kiss and a sassy howl, the dog stood wiggling while Ginny hooked up her harness for their late afternoon walk.

Unexpected events always made strolling with Jezebel an exciting experience. Their excursions were also the best way to enjoy each season in its fullest colors. As she made her way through the neighborhood, early summer blossoms wavered along the sidewalk. The gentle June breeze blew Ginny's ponytail across her face. She breathed in the fresh air, scented with the aroma of freshly cut grass. As usual, they walked at a leisurely pace because that was the only tempo Jezebel knew.

When they reached Mrs. Johnson's home, Jezebel flopped down and the older woman gifted her with a rub on her white belly. Ginny rolled the dog back onto her feet and tugged on her leash. Together, they made their way down the sidewalk in the shade of majestic century-old oaks.

Out of necessity, the walk eventually led them to the Forest Glen Historical Museum for the mysterious meeting with Annie. They circled through the group of buildings, thumping their way along the wooden boardwalk that led past an old log cabin.

Peeping in the window of the squared log structure, Ginny imagined what it would have been like to live in one room with a whole family gathered around the warm rock fireplace. A rope bed stood in the corner of the small building. A trestle table in front of the fireplace held artifacts from bygone days. Hand-dipped candles dangled from their strings on wall pegs. Drying sage and other spices adorned the bare rafters crossing the beamed ceiling. A large blackened pot hung over the ash-filled fireplace. Ginny could still smell the scent of burning wood emanating from the structure. Her students enjoyed visiting the cabin almost as much as the old train depot, where Jezebel suddenly pulled Ginny.

She strained against her leash until she reached an antique spittoon sitting on the porch of the Civil War era train depot. Upon reaching her goal, she furiously sniffed the pot. Ginny pulled back on the purple leash when the dog's pink tongue began lapping at the tobacco-stained container.

A work train rumbled down the tracks behind the depot. She watched a few stones shift in the gravel bed that lay on the same path created in the late 1830s by Forest Glen's early settlers. Her students had enjoyed learning how a team of horses once pulled the first train down those tracks until a steam engine arrived from the east.

A bearded engineer tooted the whistle. Ginny waved and Jezebel howled as the rumbling train passed. *Another bearded man,* Ginny mused, as her thoughts once again turned to the professor. Why did he keep popping up in her mind since their brief meeting? She'd heard of instant attraction before, but this was getting ridiculous. She didn't even know the guy's name. Her dream of writing and producing a musical was about to become a reality if she could get over the past and face the future without fear. Ginny had no plans to become involved with any man this summer, and this time she would be careful who she trusted as the musical came together.

Forcing herself to concentrate on the present, she continued her walk past the re-created barn, which served as a museum classroom, and then approached a steeple-topped brick building with tall windows. Smiling, she remembered the day her students attended the one-room school as 1800s students. Dressed as an old-maid schoolmarm, she taught the children a lesson involving reading from *The McGuffy Readers*. Later that day, as they sat around the gazebo in the museum's gardens, the students ate meals from lunch tins, made from large cafeteria cans.

If Ginny ever gave in to the idea of love, and found time to fall for someone, she wanted to have her wedding under the roof of that gazebo or in the historical museum's Victorian mansion. The white latticed gazebo was beautiful in winter, spring, summer, and fall. It would be the perfect place to say those sacred vows. Unexpectedly, a brief image of a bearded groom flashed through Ginny's mind. She laughed at the picture of an old-maid schoolteacher and a traveling actor as they spoke their vows under the cover of the quaint gazebo. Maybe she would write another musical, about the imagined couple.

A knock interrupted her thoughts. Ginny looked up into the kitchen window of the museum's mansion and noticed a shadowed figure waving through the backlit pane. Good, Annie was in the museum and hopefully able to answer the worries that she had caused. Ginny skirted the building and headed to the back door.

Peering through the glass-paned panel, Ginny tapped on the employee's entrance as Annie bounded down the servants' steps from the kitchen of the late 1800s home. Dressed in full Native American garb, Annie looked ready to conquer the world, wearing a bear claw necklace and sporting a bone knife secured at her waist with a woven belt. The belt wrapped around a white chemise blouse with a knee-length cotton skirt over hand-sewn leggings. A beaded leather pouch hung from her side. A metal gorget hung as a protective shield around the soft part of her throat. A wampum necklace of purple and white shell beads dangled below that, ready for business.

"Hey, am I glad to see you. I have some really good news. It looks like the county is interested in raising some support for the musical, too. Several of their council members are coming to the meeting. One of our state representatives even responded to my invitation. Do you remember the philanthropist, Edmund Bradley? He supports many arts events in this area. He's bringing a professor with him to the musical presentation. This ought to be really great! By the way, I heard the professor's single, and I'm guessing he's around your age, or slightly older. Jezebel, are you looking for your treat?" Annie paused long enough to reach into her special doggie biscuit jar.

Ginny held up her hand and grabbed the opportunity to get a word in with the talkative firebrand. "Annie! You know I'm not looking for anyone right now. Let's get back to the presentation. I thought we were only going to have a simple musical here on the grounds. A family picnic with people donating to the museum...Why do we need all these politicians and money people getting in on the act?

"I told you we're going big. It won't take much to enlarge what you've already written, into a full-blown, Broadway-style production. A few additional scenes and we can reach for the sky, or at least a stage. We can rent out an auditorium and have authentic costumes; maybe we can hire a pit orchestra, or add some dances. The ticket sales from a community musical will do more than tide us over this year. The money we raise will keep this museum open for years!"

Ginny's mouth opened, and then clamped shut. What had Annie done? They'd worked on the musical for over a year. After Ginny had written a song for the school visit with her students, Annie recruited her to write several other songs related to historical field trips and school curricula. Those songs had blended into the ninety-minute musical, created for the preservation of the museum's future. She had added a romantic twist to the plot when she realized the production would be for a larger audience. She had never dreamed it would be as big as Annie now proposed.

"But Annie, we can't possibly do this on our own."

"That's why I'm recruiting help and we're going to start by getting some political and monetary support from the people who are coming to this meeting." Annie crossed her arms and looked Ginny in the eye. "You can do this. I know you can. A little bird told me you've been doing some special music at your church. Surely you can sing in front of a few politicians."

Mention of Ginny's church reminded her of the recent prayer for strength. Her faith had grown since finding the little church in an older downtown neighborhood. The small congregation welcomed her and accepted her mother's idiosyncrasies with open arms. Singing duets with her friend, Hope, in front of loving worshippers in no way compared with trying to drag support from an unknown audience of influence. If the Forest Glen Historical Museum's future was not so uncertain, she would refuse Annie, but the museum desperately needed the funding. Annie's face looked as sad as Jezebel's drooping visage. The pleading dog and museum curator both stared at her, waiting for an answer.

Ginny sucked in a fortifying breath and tossed another of Annie's dog biscuits to Jezebel. Then she tossed her reluctant answer to Annie. "You're really going to have to help me with this event. You know I'm not thrilled about speaking to adults. I'll need your prayers, but I'll also need your backing, if I get stuck somewhere in this presentation. Maybe you should wear your outfit. It might convince someone we need a costumer." She crossed her arms and stared at Annie's clothing.

"Oh this--I just finished up a presentation for some Cub Scouts. I think they were surprised to learn that Native Americans from Ohio didn't wear feathered war bonnet headdresses and live in teepees. Now about your speech, I'll be there, but you won't need me. You'll do fine." Annie flashed a supportive grin. "You, my friend, are the talented one, and I expect to hear some singing, too."

"I'll try, but I'm a little nervous about being in front of all those politicians and dignitaries. Fourth graders are more my speed." *And college professors are way out of my league at this point.* Though she did not need to mention that to Annie and get the woman's matchmaking juices flowing.

"Then just think of them as fourth graders. Hey, you could always remember the old saying, 'Just imagine them in their underwear.'"

Definitely not a good idea when it came to full-grown men, but Ginny nodded to avoid an argument with her energetic friend.

"Right... Uh, well, if you put it that way, I guess I'll try to handle the speech. So, which room are we going to be in for the presentation?" Ginny definitely needed to change the direction of the conversation.

"I thought we'd use the parlor. That way there will be plenty of room to set up some folding chairs in the adjoining entrance hall, if we fill up the settees and upholstered seats. The old piano is there for you to play the music for us. By the way, did I tell you the professor that's coming is some kind of musical theater person?"

"No, you didn't. I'm not sure that's a very comforting thought. He may think we're amateurs, or worse. You better be prepared to jump in if he asks me something I can't handle." A fluttering case of nerves settled in her stomach at the thought of an expert in the field evaluating her musical. Though she'd been on the stage crew of a few community musicals and co-directed several elementary school pageants with Melody, the thought of a professional evaluating her play did not boost her confidence.

"I'll only help if you need me. I know you'll do fine. Now, what do you think I should fix for dessert for the meeting? I am thinking about either Grandma Nell's special brownies with melted chocolate icing, or maybe some lemon bars with sprinkles of powdered sugar. Which do you think would be better? Hey, I could do both." Annie grabbed a pen and jotted down a shopping list for things she needed for the meeting.

Ginny's mouth watered at the thought of her friend's well-known treats. After a brief discussion of drinks and goodies for the presentation, Ginny collected Jezebel and herded her toward home. As soon as the hound entered her domain, she headed for her food dish, which Ginny promptly filled. With loud chomping sounds, the basset hound sloppily devoured her food.

"Did all that talk make you hungry, girl? I guess I better find something for myself, too." Ginny looked through her frozen entrees, popped lasagna into the microwave, and began preparing a salad to go with it. Chuckling to herself, she remembered the remainder of her last salad, splattered on the strange-looking drama tie stretched down the professor's muscular chest.

A ping brought her thoughts back to the present. The aroma of Italian spices wafted through the kitchen. Ah, the joys of microwaving... Ginny made meals that were more complicated when she had the time and energy, but it was easier to use the modern convenience for one person. Grandma's cookbook mocked her from a shelf near the refrigerator. Maybe someday she'd have a family to cook for, like Annie.

Things were probably different over at Annie Brown's home, where she most likely prepared a feast for her husband and almost-grown teens. Even if the whole family wasn't there, Annie would probably prepare them a plate to dine on when they came in from their various activities and jobs. Where did that woman find her energy?

It didn't take Ginny long to finish her meal and clean up the few dishes involved. A quick shower renewed her energy. Dressed in comfy sleep shorts and an "I Love Basset Hounds" tee-shirt, she logged onto her computer. As usual, no major issues popped up in her inbox, other than a short note from Mom requesting a visit from Jezebel. Sometimes Ginny thought her mom loved the hound dog more than her own daughter. Annie preferred texting to email, so for now, all her questions and demands had been reluctantly answered. She opened a new document and began to outline her thoughts for Tuesday's meeting.

Two hours and a bag of microwave popcorn later, she had an outline in place. She had also lifted many prayers for courage and presence of mind for the upcoming meeting. Stifling a yawn, she sent Jezebel out for one more visit to the back yard. The dim light from a slivered moon and dark skies reminded her to call it a day and get some long-awaited rest. She would need every bit of energy and courage for the upcoming presentation.

Chapter 3

Ginny woke refreshed despite dreams about drama professors and musicals. Jezebel *woofed* as bright sunrays peeked through slits in curtain-clad windows. Ginny pushed the window coverings aside, which only served to highlight dust and dog hair gathered in corners of the room. Great! Just what she needed...Then again, maybe sweeping would be a good distraction from the fast-approaching meeting about her musical.

After a quick trip outside, Jezebel tackled some of the debris lurking in the corners and came up with a muzzle full of fuzz. Turning her thoughts to the task at hand, Ginny tried to sweep the dust collection into neat piles, but Jezebel only made the situation worse. The crazy hound scattered the furry mess and tasted a few samples of "dust bunny" along the way. The rambunctious beast twisted in glee as she chased an airborne piece of fluff. Legs, tail, and drool flew as the surprised hound spun on the polished floor and toppled the tote Ginny had left sitting by the door. Papers flew from the school bag that formerly rested against the wall. The drama camp flyer skittered across smooth hardwood planks. Jezebel chomped the paper between her teeth. She shook her head as drool covered the flyer. The professor's smiling countenance looked up from what was left of the advertisement.

Ginny rescued the errant pieces of paper and gave the drama flyer a second look. She should probably just throw it away. Or, perhaps she could use him as an inspiration for a character in some future writing. Too bad the flier was in black and white. It would be interesting to know what color his eyes were. Ridiculous. She needed to quit wasting time on some unknown guy, even if he did look like a hunk. She had better things to think about. Maybe she should go ahead and contact the Russell family to see if they would let her send Melissa to the drama camp. Acting could be a way to help the shy student gain confidence. She smoothed the paper and laid it on her desk. Did the wrinkled paper make it look like he winked? Nice.

Picking up her cell, she dialed Melissa's foster parents. The phone rang twice before Ginny heard Melissa's tentative voice. "You've reached the Russell home, this is Melissa."

"Hi, sweetheart, this is Miss Cline. How are you doing?"

"I'm okay. I miss school already. Do you want to come visit?" The youngster's voice grew stronger as she spoke into the phone.

"I will visit you sometime very soon. Would you ask Mrs. Russell to get on the phone? I have something I want to ask both of you."

"Sure." The noise of a telephone receiver clattering on a hard surface traveled through the phone line.

Moments later, Chelsea Russell's cheery voice joined the conversation as Ginny proposed the idea of sending Melissa to the drama camp.

"That sounds like a fantastic idea. What do you think, Melissa?" Chelsea asked.

"I'm not sure. I might be scared if I don't know anyone," the child responded slowly.

"If it's all right with Mrs. Russell, maybe I can come with you for a while on the first day and introduce you to some of the other students. There may even be someone from our class this year that you would know." A long silence greeted Ginny and then a hesitant *yes* came from Melissa. Chelsea quickly agreed to the arrangement and offered to join them in their journey to the camp.

Ginny returned to her chores with a bounce in her step and a zip in her dusting. As lunchtime neared, she decided she deserved more than a frozen meal. She searched the kitchen bookshelf and reached for the tattered cookbook, inherited from her grandmother. She flipped through the book until she found an old family recipe pasted onto a blank page near the back. Thoughts of Grandma's sauce made her mouth water.

She thawed two chicken breasts, while she whipped up the family recipe for lemon-dill sauce. Everything went into the oven with a baked potato. Last year's frozen veggies shared from Mrs. Johnson's backyard bounty of broccoli, mild red peppers and zucchini would make a perfect stir-fry. She just needed to get them from the freezer in preparation for frying them at the right time. When zesty chicken aromas floated from the oven, she heated the oil, and soon vegetables sizzled.

She savored the tasty meal. It was better than she remembered. Nearly as good as when Grandma fixed it! Too bad Mom never learned to cook like her. At least Ginny had learned a few things about cooking during extended summer visits. Sloppy chewing and slurping sounds interrupted her happy thoughts of pleasant days spent on her grandparents' farm. Jezebel looked up briefly and then lowered her speckled head and ears into her bowl, gulping down her portion of the chicken, minus the spicy sauce. After a satisfied shake of her wrinkled body, the canine plopped down for her afternoon nap. Ginny placed the empty dog dish in the sink and headed outside to do some yard work.

Sweat dripped down Ginny's brow as she mowed grass in the hot afternoon sun. Then she pulled some weeds from flowerbeds scattered around her small yard. There was nothing ladylike about doing yard chores, but the invading weeds demanded attention as she tackled the weekly chore. She had no other help than Jezebel, who managed to uproot more plant life than the average dog. As temperatures rose, Ginny decided to check out the neighborhood pool for a little cool down--after she sent Jezebel out for one more trot around the backyard.

A call to the pool office provided the information that family swim would be over at seven and adult swim would begin soon after. Ginny opted to swim at the later time to avoid dealing with a crowd of students who probably already missed their teacher. Donning her modest one-piece lavender swimsuit, covered by a pink shorts outfit, she set out for the aquatic park. The neighborhood pool was only a few blocks away, so Ginny walked. Her flip-flops slapped out a rhythmic beat as she made her way down the street. Singing her *Friend of a Friend* song from the musical filled her heart with hope and added a bounce to her steps.

A butterfly fluttered across her path and she paused to watch it light on a flowering azalea bush at the edge of a nicely manicured lawn. Ginny pulled out her phone and snapped a picture of the colorful insect perched on the glowing bush, located in front of the beautifully restored home. The white home with green shutters was an older structure with possible connections to the Underground Railroad. Ginny had read about the lovely old building in her research for the musical. Rumors had circulated about a hidden room located either in its attic or basement. Renovations throughout the home's history had made it impossible to know if such a room ever existed, but the townsfolk liked to ponder the possibilities hidden in the home's past.

The building's history paralleled the lore surrounding the Woodson House, which Ginny had used in the musical. The house she stood adoring had recently been for sale, but her limited resources put an end to the temptation to buy it. Her little cottage was good enough for now.

The former owner had taken pride in the home's suggested history and had created a beautiful array of flowers and shrubbery in the yard and around the house. The ancient boxwoods had stood guard over the entrance to the backyard English garden for as long as people could remember. Ginny wondered if the new owner would maintain the beauty of the garden. She certainly hoped so, and snapped another picture as the butterfly flew away.

Hearing the front door of the house open, Ginny scurried on her way toward the pool. Out of the corner of her eye she saw a tall, masculine figure with a green towel around his neck make his way down the steps and through the flowered lawn. Great, she thought, *I hope he didn't see me taking pictures of his flowers and now it looks like he's headed for the pool, too.* A cheery whistle confirmed her suspicions as she hurried up the sidewalk without a backward glance.

She welcomed the distraction of paying her entrance fee to the pool and zipped into the ladies' locker room for the required shower. One of these years, she should get a pool membership card, but not this one, since she had no idea how busy her summer would be. Right now, though, it was time to relax and she planned to do just that. She grabbed her gear and entered the pool area. A white plastic chair near the deep end provided a place to lay her towel. A couple of brisk laps would be just the thing to take her mind off any other thoughts. Sliding into the cool water, she shivered as her body adjusted to the temperature change and then began to swim across the pool at a fast tempo.

After several laps, Ginny slowed her pace and relished floating gently through the water, on her back. Looking at the blue sky was so calming. A few white puffy clouds floated across the azure expanse. God sure made it beautiful this time of year. *The heavens declare the glory of God,* flowed through her mind as she glided along.

Ker-splash!

The wake of a careless diver's belly flop obliterated her view of the sky. She sputtered out a mouthful of water. Rotating to her front, she quickly swam toward the edge of the pool to pull herself back together. What a way to break such a peaceful moment.

"Need a towel, flower lady?" a warm bass voice asked, as a man's muscular arm held out a towel in a familiar shade of green. The sandy hair on his arm sparkled in the early summer evening's sunlight. She paused a second too long before she shook her head, and tried to make her tongue work its way into a sensible reply .

"No thanks, uh... I'll be fine."

A fresh masculine scent emanated from the refused towel as Ginny cautiously eyed its owner. She took a long, studied glimpse of the well-built man who owned the flowered historical home. The sun glistened off his damp hair and skin as his full lips grinned in a quirky but friendly manner. Dimples winked at Ginny from what appeared to be freshly shaven face. She forced a smile as heat filled her cheeks. He had seen her admiring his flowers. She quickly made her way into the middle of the pool and swam a few more vigorous laps.

He was a tall man with reddish blonde hair and a trim physique. But Ginny wasn't about to introduce herself to a stranger at a pool, even one who acted chivalrous. A girl had to be careful who she trusted these days. She dismissed the thought that there was something familiar about her would-be rescuer. Instead, she tried concentrating on swimming as she flutter-kicked her way across the pool.

Rotating to her back again and hoping for no more careless divers, she wondered if his eyes were blue like the sky. Now, where had that idea come from? Too many thoughts about eyes lately... Eyes could be deceiving. James's eyes had certainly been full of lies. No need to look for trouble. She'd better forget that train of thought and enjoy her swim while she had the chance. As her distracted mind turned to the musical, she slowed her swim strokes to match the beat of the tunes that danced across the stage of her thoughts.

♥ ♥ ♥

Scott Hallmark stood by the pool and watched the beautiful brunette paddle her way across the blue water with a smooth grace that was easy on the eyes. If his eyes didn't deceive him, she resembled the same dynamo who nearly mowed him down when he delivered flyers to Forest Glen Elementary. He prayed the students had gotten the information. His thoughts turned from the flyers and back to the graceful swimmer. Scott reached up to rub his freshly shaven chin in contemplation. He welcomed the change in texture, now that the church drama had ended and his summer routine had started. He preferred a smooth chin over a grizzly one for the warmer months. A breeze filled with sun lotion and chlorine blew across his bare face while his eyes searched the waters for a splash of lavender. He wondered if the lady in question hadn't recognized him from their brief encounter without his wooly face covering.

A part of him wished they could meet again with a proper introduction--maybe after her swim. But then again, life was hectic right now. The chiming sound of his phone reinforced that thought. After a quick glance at the ID, he paused before opening Edmund's call. The man had been trying all week to schedule a meeting about that new project. He needed to answer this time and get the dreaded conversation out of the way. He shuddered....as his phone made the connection.

"Hey, Edmund. How can I help you?"

Edmond rattled on for several minutes about a musical he was considering funding. The stunning swimmer who continued to make laps in the pool distracted Scott's attention, until the man asked, "Do you think you could meet with me tonight to discuss your involvement? I really need someone who knows what they're doing who can oversee this project. Carl's coffee shop is open until 11:00 and I doubt you have any conflicts this time of night." Edmund's tone suggested there wasn't a choice about meeting.

"Sure, I'd be glad to meet you in an hour." Scott sighed. No relaxation tonight. "Did you say some local has written this musical? Are you sure it's quality work? I don't want to commit to something without knowing a few more details." Amateurs wanting to be stars had knocked at his door more than once and the results had not been pretty.

Scott gathered his things and slid into his shoes as he ended the conversation with his wealthy patron. As usual, it seemed like any time he started to have interest in a woman, work always interfered. He'd had a few dates over the years, but most women resented the late evening rehearsal schedules a career in drama demanded. Or the woman used his influence at work to gain something she wanted. He needed to remind Edmund that the demands of the camp and college responsibilities did not allow him the leisure to take on a poor-quality project. The man probably expected Scott to be a miracle worker. He'd rather spend time watching the shapely mermaid make her way through the sparkling pool water. Maybe he would see her again, since it appeared she lived close enough to walk to the pool.

His dreams of holding a tenure track position at a faith-based college had finally arrived. If everything went as planned, he would be on his way to earning full tenure at Freedom College. Years spent gaining experience in non-tenure track positions and in theaters across the planet weren't very conducive to relationships. However, if he did well in his new position that would all change.

He slipped the green towel around his neck and left the pool area after one more glimpse of his mystery woman. Maybe one day soon, he could start thinking about the possibility of meeting someone special like the pretty woman zipping across the pool. As soon as that thought swam through his mind, he crossed it off. It would not be wise to lose focus on his goals, especially if he got pulled into Edmund's little scenario on top of work and the summer camp.

♥♥♥

Later that evening, as Ginny lounged in bed reading a Christian romance, her thoughts drifted again to the owner of the green towel. Did he resemble the hero in her book? He reminded her of someone, but she couldn't place who. She'd not planned to blush, but her cheeks warmed when he held out that towel. At least the incident had taken her mind off the disaster in the school hallway. Too much fiction and fantasy filled her mind these days. Although that wasn't exactly a bad thing. Her vivid imagination had helped her create her musical, after all, and that little exercise would hopefully benefit the museum.

Enough--she needed to rein in her wayward thoughts and read her chapter from the Bible before calling it a night. The only man she could really trust lived in her heart as her Savior. She needed to be thinking about Jesus right now, not some fictional hero.

As she stretched out on her bed and read the fourth chapter of Philippians, she claimed the promise of the thirteenth verse. With Christ's help, she could do anything. She would make a great presentation on Tuesday, or at least do her best. At least she could promise to try. She'd do whatever it took to put the musical together for the sake of Annie, the community, and the historical village. She definitely needed God's help. She fervently pleaded in her prayers that everything would work together for good. God's restful peace drowned her worries about the presentation. Laying it all at the Lord's feet, she fell asleep dreaming about songs of freedom and sky-blue eyes. They were blue!

Chapter 4

The following Tuesday, Ginny found herself staring into an ornate mirror at the museum. The image reflected a confident woman. If only that were the case. Ginny swallowed. Just the day before, her Memorial Day holiday had wavered between near panic to prayerful petitions. An errant curl formed on her damp forehead. She pressed it back into place and struggled to find the small tube of hair gel, lost in the depths of her purse. Another tendril tickled its way down her neck as she shivered. Backing away from the pink marble pedestal sink in the museum's antique bathroom, she paced the short length of the small boudoir. Concentrate. She shouldn't be worried about the presentation. Right? Only God could help her. That's where she placed her trust. What happened to last night's peace?

As a professional teacher, she knew all about persuading students to learn, so why did her thoughts turn to walking out the back door and forgetting her dreams for the musical and the museum? She needed help, and she needed it fast. She plopped down on the wrought iron ice cream parlor-style chair near the sink and closed her eyes.

Give me strength, Lord. With Your help I can find the courage to do this. Show me a way to calm this attack of nerves. Ginny blew out a shaky breath and opened her eyes as a drop of water fell with a plop onto a porcelain surface. She laughed at what sat right in front of her. Metallic lion paws held up an enormous tub with archaic hardware, sparking her imagination. The Lion of God had provided a humorous distraction. Maybe a quick swim in the claw-footed bathtub would cool her off. Her mind flittered back to the green towel man at the pool. She needed a good splash in the face. She quickly blotted her forehead with a wet tissue and hummed the tune to her *Freedom Song.*

Praising the Lord for little distractions, Ginny made a funny face at herself as she touched up her pale pink lip gloss. The comic reflection in the beveled mirror bolstered her courage and she whispered a final prayer for strength.

"Hey Ginny, are you okay in there?" Annie's muffled tones vibrated through the oak door.

"Just getting myself wound up for the presentation..." Ginny's voice shook, despite her effort to control it.

"I hope you mean in a good way. You've got fifteen minutes before you're on, so gather your courage and get out here."

Ginny pushed the door open and fell into one of Annie's warm hugs. The woman's scent of cinnamon and chocolate drops wrapped her in confidence. They linked arms and walked toward the parlor of the old mansion, turned museum headquarters. Warmth spread through Ginny's veins. With God and Annie on her side, what could go wrong?

At least she had the foresight to check the old upright piano over the weekend. Plunking on its ancient keys provided strident tones worthy of a twentieth century Philip Glass prepared piano composition. Thank the Lord, she had converted the music into midi files on her computer. At least that potential disaster had been averted through the modern miracle of computerized sound.

Ginny released Annie's arm and stepped into the room. She concentrated on making her way to a music stand located near a small marble-faced fireplace. Her laptop sat nearby on the piano bench and woke easily when she tapped the keyboard. Icons for each of the songs flashed on the desktop screen in the precise order needed. Another worry cast aside.

Still, she kept her gaze down, studying the intricate designs on the painted canvas floor covering as she pushed an extension cord to the side. All she needed would be to trip over a wire. Maybe she could hold on to God's strength longer if she didn't look at her audience before starting. She knew better, though. Eye contact reached out to people, and staring at her shoes would not convince anyone to support the musical.

The front door to the museum scraped open, drawing Ginny's attention as several people entered the mansion's foyer. She relaxed when she recognized Grace Cole, parent of a former student, entering with a friendly wave. Grace now served on Forest Glen's City Council. It would be nice to have a familiar face in the group.

Mayor Kyle seemed friendly enough when he joined the crowd and introduced several members of the county council. Annie flitted from one person to another, chattering about anything and everything. Everyone enjoyed Annie's brownies and lemon bars. Not Ginny, though. Butterflies fluttered in her stomach as the clock hands edged closer to the top of the hour. Everyone, including the state representative, milled around, waiting on the arrival of Edmund Bradley and his professor friend. Ginny selfishly found herself praying they would be blessed and the professor wouldn't make it. She chewed on her lip, and exchanged a look with Annie, who gave her a thumbs up sign from across the room.

Annie encouraged the group to take a seat as she took her place at the front of the room. "Welcome, everyone. I am so glad you all could come to this meeting. I think you will be thoroughly delighted by what we are about to share. I hope each of your groups will be able to lend support to this effort in some way. My friend, Ginny, spent the last year and a half researching and creating a wonderful musical about our area's involvement with the Underground Railroad. This musical has possibilities for expanding into a full-blown Broadway-style musical. I have full confidence that Ginny has the ability to put this program together for our community. *Incident at Woodson House* will also serve as a venue to fund the future of our museum. She is one of my favorite volunteers and local educators. Please welcome Ginny Cline."

Ginny swallowed and carefully straightened her outline on the mahogany music stand next to her computer. She glanced at her audience as the entry door squeaked open one more time. Two gentlemen entered as she tried to make her mouth move. Recognition of the well-known philanthropist, Edmund Bradley, filtered through Ginny's trembling thoughts. Following him could only be the mysterious theater professor, the man who might have the power to destroy any dreams of her community musical.

Annie Brown's welcome of the stragglers offered Ginny a much-needed reprieve. A trickle of perspiration formed on her forehead where another tendril of hair escaped its binding. Not only did she face the feared professor, but he was one and the same as the green towel man from the pool and owner of the much-adored neighborhood house. Breathing deeply to calm her racing heart, Ginny plastered what she hoped was a confident smile upon her face and casually brushed the loose lock of hair back into place. She nodded to the latecomers and pushed her distracted thoughts from her mind. A raised eyebrow over a very blue pair of eyes acknowledged the tall man's recognition of Ginny. So the eyes were blue. Ginny momentarily forgot about the presentation as she stared into the captivating face.

The sound of chairs scraping on the wooden floor drew her attention to the audience, who turned to Ginny in anticipation. Annie poked her with a not-so-subtle elbow to the ribs before taking a seat on the front row. The moment had come to conquer her fears and rely on God's strength. She cleared her throat, doused her doubt with a quick sip of water, and then stumbled though the introductory sentences about *Incident at Woodson House*.

"Our area has a rich historical connection to the Underground Railroad. Citizens of Forest Glen were active in reaching out to many travelers on their way to freedom from slavery. Our historical museum is a valuable resource for keeping our past alive. A year ago, Annie asked me to consider sharing a part of that history through song and I agreed to write a musical. Annie is hoping we can grow the musical into a community theater event, which will gain some much-needed financial freedom for the Forest Glen Historical Museum."

Annie's face gleamed with hope when she smiled.

Ginny's voice grew stronger as she shared her passion for the historical presentation through music. "The 1840s setting for our production is based on research from documents found at the museum. That valuable information provided proof that the area surrounding Forest Glen boasted several homes which were stations on the Underground Railroad. One of those homes, the Woodson House, still stands today, thanks to efforts by the museum to have it declared a heritage site. Our story will feature a family of runaways seeking refuge with the Woodsons on their way north to freedom."

Ginny reached over to the computer and clicked the first musical icon. Warm tones flowed from the speakers as her voice caught and then formed the words for the first song. "We're heading north to dreams of freedom..." Ginny's voice filled the small room as she closed her eyes and pictured the wayfarers passing through Forest Glen. When her last notes faded away, she opened her eyes. They focused first on the professor's unmoving mask. No reaction--Edmund, however, beamed and started a round of applause.

Encouraged, Ginny continued her speech. Joy strengthened her resolve. "Not everyone in town favored the Underground Railroad. Laws made it illegal to help slaves escape. Anyone caught aiding runaways faced going to jail. It took courage to be a 'friend of a friend,' which was a code word for those who would help the refugees, and the title of my next song."

Ginny forced her gaze to meet Edmund's as she sang, "A friend of a friend is a friend to the end. A friend shows that they really care..."

The song served several purposes in her life. For the musical, it spoke of being willing to give a life for those traveling on the Underground Railroad. She had taught the song's concept to her students at school in an effort to encourage being friends to everyone, regardless of who they were or where they came from. Children in her small Sunday school class learned the words when she taught about Christ's sacrifice on the cross. As the music faded, Ginny's heart filled with gratitude for a supportive friend like Annie, who pushed her to create *Incident at Woodson House.*

"Our musical is fiction, but it is based on what might have happened during a weeklong game of hide-and-seek, with a wily slave catcher trying to find the runaways."

As she sang a sampling of each song, her confidence grew, but not enough to look in the professor's direction again. She imagined that he sat there analyzing her less than perfect voice. She brushed those worries aside and concentrated on the crucial presentation. God seemed to be providing her with both courage and voice, and she pushed herself to keep the momentum going.

As the virtually flawless presentation drew near its conclusion, a thrill of newfound confidence flowed in Ginny's veins. A final click turned on the accompaniment music for the song where a man from Forest Glen realized he needed to help the runaways get safely out of town. In doing so, he broke down the final barrier keeping him from the woman he loved.

"I'll give my life to save the lost; I know I must what e'er the cost..."

Ginny looked heavenward and released her last note, fighting the tears that often accompanied singing the song. Only Christ had that kind of love for her. No man in her life could match the dedication she'd created in her musical hero. Her good friend Annie supported this musical and needed the help for the museum. The hour had come to find out if her presentation had been worth the effort.

"Annie Brown encouraged me throughout the creation of this project, and she thought each of you might be interested in hearing about it. I hope you will consider some kind of financial support for the *Incident at Woodson House*, whether for a simple outdoor presentation or a major stage production. Thank you very much for listening. Do you have any questions?"

As several moments of silence prevailed, Ginny grasped the stand and desperately glanced Annie's way. Annie raised her shoulders and shifted in her seat. Ginny chanced a look at the professor and saw only deep concentration, which revealed nothing. She swallowed and looked around the room for any indication of acceptance or rejection. Annie finally rose to her feet and looked as if she was about to say something--anything.

Then Mayor Kyle broke the silence. He slapped his leg and grinned from ear to ear. "This is great! Can you imagine the publicity the town will get if we pull this thing off? I vote for a full-fledged production. This venture will put us on the map for sure."

"We've been trying to boost tourism in this area for several years. This may be just what we need," added David Ericson, a council member.

Several voices joined in with ideas for promoting the area and its history. Would the newspapers provide coverage for events associated with the musical? Perhaps they could pair the musical with the annual Fall Fest. Maybe the churches could get involved.

"But who is going to pay for a full-fledged production?"

All eyes turned to the professor, whose strong voice had managed to carry over the din.

"I'm sure we can manage something," Mayor Kyle answered as he proudly placed his hand on his chest and then swung it out to indicate the gathered group. "Just how much do you think it would cost to put this thing on, Miss Cline?"

Ginny wrung her hands and stuttered out a staggering figure, based on her research with a local amateur theater group.

The mayor smiled. "No problem here. I'll bring it up at the next council meeting."

Nodding heads of city and county council members brought a flood of relief to Ginny as her hands slowly relaxed at her sides. Even the state representative indicated there might be money available through the state arts council. Ginny and Annie shared a smile of victory before turning to thank their benefactors.

"It won't be enough." Once again, the professor's commanding voice put a damper on the swelling tide of positive comments.

Ginny glared at the man. Just who did he think he was, anyway? The mayor obviously thought the same thing, since he voiced Ginny's unspoken question aloud.

"I'm Dr. Scott Hallmark. I'll be teaching musical theater at the college starting this fall. I've directed many productions, and if you want to do this right, you'll need four times the funds requested."

Ginny's heart thudded in her chest. How would they ever come up with that kind of money? She reached for a glass of water as her mouth suddenly dried out. Now the man dared to take away the dream that Ginny and Annie had worked so hard on for more than a year? Another dream-stealing man...

Voices mumbled in the back of the room and the chairman of the county council stood. "I'll see if the county is interested in matching what the city has to offer."

Ginny let go of the breath she hadn't realized she held.

Grace Cole chimed in, "I'm also on the hospital auxiliary. There are funds available for community grants. I'm pretty sure I can convince our group to make a nice donation."

Annie couldn't resist doing a little victory dance in the background. Ginny gave in to the joy and sent a victorious look in the stoic professor's direction, daring him to object to their apparent success. As blue eyes met green, a warm feeling of another kind flooded Ginny and she quickly broke the connection to concentrate on the celebration going on around her.

Once again, many voices sounded as other participants mentioned agencies in the community that might be able to grant monies to the program. Before long, it looked like they were going to be well on their way toward raising the amount that Professor Hallmark suggested they would need. Ginny's hopes rose as she met Annie's triumphant expression.

Edmund Bradley made his way through the crowd and heartily shook hands with Annie and Ginny. "This looks like a very interesting project. I've been thinking during the last few minutes, Annie. If the offer still holds, I'd like to help the museum produce the musical. I might even be able to find funds needed to cover what the community doesn't supply, so our doubting professor can be happy. Scott knows his stuff, though, and I'm glad he came to the meeting, aren't you?"

Before Ginny could answer negatively, Annie deftly changed the subject by inquiring how the two men had met.

"Scott asked my foundation to consider funding a summer camp. I checked him out and found that he is one of the best theater people in our area. Though he is new to town, he has quite a resume that includes productions all over the country, and even a few out of the country. I had no problem funding his summer program, and when I heard about your little project, I suggested he should come here today."

"Thanks," Ginny replied, hoping her response sounded heartfelt rather than sarcastic. Her heart had taken several swift elevator rides during the last few minutes, courtesy of the confusing professor, so she failed to share Edmund's enthusiasm. When she turned to a warm touch on her shoulder and found herself looking directly into Scott Hallmark's azure eyes, she experienced another plunge into depths of confusion. Seeking a distraction, she looked down and focused on the floral patterned rug covering part of the hardwood floor. Then the man opened his mouth again.

"I hope you understand that I only wanted to help. Years in this business told me you would need more financial support. I had to speak up. You'll be glad for the extra money if these organizations come through for you. Good luck with your program. It won't be an easy journey." Scott smiled at Ginny with a hopeful look that seemed to go beyond his concerns for the musical.

Ginny glared at the smiling man. "Thanks, I'm sure you'll provide us with all kinds of helpful advice."

She was sure that some of her sarcasm must have come through this time, because the professor raised those interesting sandy eyebrows and coolly excused himself after commenting, "No thank you. I have enough other projects to keep me busy, including my theater camp." Sliding on his pair of dark sunglasses, the intimidating man stalked from the room.

As Ginny watched the retreating professor, she breathed a sigh of relief, and then it struck her. Without the beard, she hadn't recognized that not only was he the man at the pool, he was also the person she had run into in the hall at school. His dark glasses and mention of the theater camp had been the last clues to finally unmasking the identity of the man. Too bad his good looks didn't make up for his bossy opinions about funding her musical.

She pushed those thoughts out of her mind and began shaking the hands of her newfound supporters. She found it hard to believe, but it looked like their dream had a chance of coming to fruition. As the crowd thinned, Ginny finally made her way to Annie's dessert table and celebrated by sampling a small brownie and lemon bar. When the last politician stepped out the door, she collapsed into a nervous heap of exhaustion. Ginny patted the chair next to her and invited Annie to sit for a few minutes.

"I couldn't have done that alone, Annie. God sure took care of my knocking knees today, and you are truly the best friend anyone could ever have."

"I knew you could do it. Now we just have to hope and pray that all the funding comes through." Annie gave her a reassuring pat on the arm.

"We'll get enough. I doubt we'll need as much as Mr. High and Mighty Professor thinks we need." Ginny crossed her arms as irritation fueled her thoughts of the domineering man. "I'll be happy if we get enough to have a simple musical here on the museum grounds." She still preferred a small production, but if funding came through for something bigger, she would do her part.

"Well, you never know." Annie waved her hands in the air. "Just imagine what we could do if everyone comes through with their support. We'd create authentic costumes and a great set. We could even rent a big stage here in town, and have an orchestra or a pit band."

"Annie, now you are scaring me. I wouldn't know how to write for an orchestra. I just figured we'd put the play on here and use a keyboard with maybe some drums or a guitar."

"Don't worry, we'll figure it out. Just dream big and let your faith accept whatever the future brings. After all, it looks like you conquered your fear of speaking to the adults that were here for the presentation. The time has come for you to step out of your shell, because I have a feeling we are definitely going big."

"I'll try."

"Miracles can happen. I think I saw one tonight. Now, do you want to take some of these brownies home with you?" Annie offered her a plate of goodies and a friendly hug.

"Thanks, but no thanks. I'd eat too many and I don't think Jezebel needs to sink her teeth into them, either. She got really sick the last time she guzzled down too much chocolate." Ginny felt proud of her ability to pass up the calorie-laden treats, knowing she would walk an extra mile every day this week to make up for the ones she'd already consumed during the last few moments.

After cleaning up the historical village's mansion, the two women parted ways with enthusiastic congratulations on a job well done. Annie carried home most of the leftover brownies for her brood. Ginny finally agreed to bring home one lemon bar to split in celebration with Jezebel. She hoped the hound would survive the small treat without any adverse effects. As she made her way home, Ginny found her mind wandering to the professor who both intrigued and irritated her. Her traitor heart hoped she would see the attractive man again--just not at any event involving her precious dream, *Incident at Woodson House*.

Chapter 5

The next morning Scott tossed back the ancient quilt that entangled his body. Better wake up and start the day. Visions of a certain brown-haired woman were sure to torment him if he closed his eyes again. What a dreamer! A full musical with only a few community dollars? Hah! That would never happen unless the woman worked a miracle. Yawning, he rolled to his side and his cheek met his dog Carlos's wet nose.

Yip, yip. Tiny toenails pranced over Scott's arm, bounced off the bed, and then rattled across hardwood floors. So much for staying in bed for another few minutes. He rolled to a sitting position and stretched his arms overhead. Where had he put the leash? Oh yeah, right by his pair of well-worn running shoes. One of these days, he needed to fix the ancient fence that surrounded his back yard. Chihuahua-sized holes gaped from several patches of rusty fencing as the little dog took care of business. Both man and beast welcomed the early morning air, filling their lungs with deep breaths and sniffs as they explored the back yard together. Calling Carlos into the house a short time later, he checked his calendar. He needed to meet his grad assistant for final drama camp preparations at nine. Now, where had he put the coffee?

No coffee! Scott scanned his nearly empty cabinets and located a lumpy packet of instant hot chocolate hidden behind a salt shaker. Chocolate laced with the last of his milk would have to do. He stirred chalky lumps into a cup and put it in the microwave to heat. Now where did he put the last protein bars? He'd totally forgotten to stop for groceries last night. It looked like a bowl of dry cereal would be his only choice, unless he doused it in the hot drink. Hmmm--time to experiment. He chuckled as he pulled the chocolate from the microwave and covered the cereal. His focus definitely seemed off.

He couldn't believe Edmund wanted to throw money behind the cute little woman and her grandiose plan. He plopped down at his table and let his mind wander as he consumed the odd-tasting food. Those green eyes framed by long, dark lashes had probably taken in his benefactor. He'd fallen for that trick before. He shook his head at the direction his mind had taken, and gulped down the last bite of cereal laced with hot chocolate. He needed to concentrate on getting to his last preparation meeting before drama camp started next week.

Scott headed for the door as his mind once again strayed to the confusing lady from the evening before. Maybe one of these days he would have another chance to make a better impression on the interesting woman. One that did not involve him with her musical... Praying for God's help in making decisions for the day and for his possible love life, Scott whistled as he made his way to the sidewalk and walked toward the college campus. Without thinking, his whistling rang out one of her tunes from the night before. The melodies were catchy, but did she have the chops to write a good script? He didn't want to be stuck rewriting useless lines while trying to make a name for himself at the college. Still, she seemed genuine for the most part. Yep, his thoughts had definitely headed off in the wrong direction.

♥ ♥ ♥

Woof, woof, baaoooh! Warm doggie breath blew across Ginny's face as Jezebel lay her head on her owner's chest and wiggled in anticipation of an outdoor trip.

"Morning already?"

Jezebel lumbered off the bed, waddled closer to the bedroom door, and howled once more. Summer vacation had arrived, but someone forgot to tell the barking dog. Dawning light barely filtered through her curtains and her wacky hound wanted out. Whines signaled the need to hurry. This must be the penalty for the late-night lemon bar celebration. That celebration continued when she shared the news with her friends. Melody and Kara had both been thrilled to hear about the musical over the phone last night. Their calls kept her talking late into the evening, making it even harder now to clear the sleep from her eyes as she yawned and Jezebel paced.

Forcing herself out of bed, Ginny stretched and stood upright. Peeking out her bedroom window curtains, she praised the Lord as she observed a glowing sunrise spreading pink-streaked light across the morning sky. When the hound woofed another frantic bark from the bedroom door, Ginny slipped on flip-flops and hurried to obey Jezebel's nature call.

"Come on, dog, time to go out."

At the word "out," Jezebel began her happy dance down the hall, past the kitchen, and out the laundry room door. The dog's white-tipped tail whipped from side to side. Her nails drummed on the wooden deck stretching across the back of the house.

Ginny stood at the backdoor and yawned as she watched Jezebel travel around the fenced yard. Glorious pinks, purples, and blues filled the dawning skies with pastel colors. *What a beautiful morning the Lord has made! God is so good.* Grape-scented iris filled the air with their aroma as she surveyed her green lawn, refreshed by an overnight rain.

It looked like the musical might make it without any help from the frustrating professor, who kept interrupting her daydreams. Though she hated to admit it, some of her dreams during last night's tossing and turning were filled with the blue-eyed professor. The petunia bed had started to bloom and Jezebel grazed on the surrounding grass. Oh no, better get that dog in.

"Come on, girl, you're not a cow. How about having a doggie bone instead?"

Paws padded their way to the back door as the petunia-cheeked hound responded to the suggestion of a treat. Ginny filled the dog's food dish and Jezebel began to fill her tummy with kibble. Slapping up liquid refreshment from her water dish added to the happy sounds of a satisfied hound.

Ginny hummed several favorite songs from church while she prepared whole-wheat toast and fruit for her breakfast. A dab of Annie's homemade jam went perfectly with the toast. A glass of milk completed Ginny's breakfast. Jezebel finished her own meal and pranced by Ginny's feet, hoping to capture any falling crumbs. As the dog's soulful eyes followed Ginny's consumption, the beast whined until her owner rewarded the panting pet with a toasty crust.

Jezebel gulped down the bread in two chomps and then the grinning dog left the table in search of another drink from her water dish. Ginny laughed when she reached across her table and pulled the page from her verse a day calendar. It revealed Philippians 4:13. "I can do all things through Christ who strengtheneth me." The same verse she'd studied the other day. God was certainly trying to tell her something she needed to hear.

"I'll try, Lord. I know with Your help I can do anything. I really need this musical to succeed for the museum. I also want *Incident at Woodson House* to teach the community their history and show them how faith in God inspired people of long ago, as it can today. I want them to enjoy seeing some entertainment doesn't have to be rated above a G." Ginny continued with her morning devotions, giving praise and asking for God's assistance in the many aspects of her life and in the lives of those she knew.

Ginny and Jezebel spent the rest of the morning continuing their quest to end the world of dust bunnies. Jezebel bounced around in circles when Ginny brought out the sweeper. For some unknown reason, the beast loved having her fur vacuumed with the hose attachment. Ginny gave in to the dog's wishes several times, as she attempted to clean. Vacuuming and dusting were not at the top of her list during the school year, so she found plenty to do.

Annie's phone call around noon brought news that the city council would meet Thursday night. "Can you make it this coming Monday night, too? We've been invited to present at the county meeting that night."

"Thanks, Annie... I think. I'm still not real thrilled about speaking to all these adult groups."

"You'll do fine. You held their attention last night. Consider it a re-run of what you did yesterday."

"I suppose. I still can't believe we got some support."

"Well, we did, and I know you will do well at the next two meetings. Hey, why don't we ride together since parking might be limited at both places? I'll give you a pep talk on the way."

"That sounds like a good idea. I'll drive since I will need to bring some things for the presentation."

Nervous energy flowed through her veins. Pacing in her small house held no appeal, even though she found herself doing that very thing without thinking. Cleaning the rest of the house seemed out of the question. She needed some fresh air and exercise. Taking Jezebel for a walk would be a perfect outlet, if she could convince the dog to give up her nap. Waking up the slumbering beast, however, proved interesting, since Jezebel usually slept most of the early afternoon. Pulling the harness around the basset's dead weight, Ginny finally dragged the reluctant hound into a standing position and out the door.

Meandering down the sidewalk did not match what Ginny had in mind. But it seemed to be the only pace Jezebel could handle for now. At least it proved to be better than being inside with the sweeper and dust rag. Moving down the tree-lined street brought a sense of freedom as she waved to neighbors and acquaintances. It felt nice to set her own schedule for a change, even if it did have to move at the speed of a loping basset hound--who suddenly sped up. What was the dog after? Jezebel snuffed the air, gave a quick bark, and began trotting jauntily along the path at a very un-basset-like speed.

"What's gotten into you, Jezebel?" Ginny ran to keep up with the scrambling beast.

As they neared the familiar flower-edged lawn of the professor, Ginny found out what captivated Jezebel. A welcoming *yap, yap,* greeted the howling hound as she propelled her owner forward. Tethered to a post in the middle of the yard, a vocal male Chihuahua danced a welcoming tribute. His shiny black and tan coat contrasted with the brilliant green grass of the well-manicured yard. He put on quite a show for Jezebel, who seemed to lap up the attention as she panted for the little dog.

"Hey there, cutie," Ginny called out to the bouncing canine.

"Well hello, Ginny," came back the answer in a now familiar bass voice that implied he heard her address his dog, and had teasingly accepted the compliment as his own.

Ginny's attention flickered from the yapping dog to his owner. Butterflies fluttered in her chest. Just what she needed, another rollercoaster ride courtesy of the professor... She felt her heart pick up its pace as Scott Hallmark stood up from behind a nearby bush with a gardening trowel in one hand and a bedding tray of flowers in the other. A lock of tawny hair hanging down on his forehead added to the charm of the appealing guy. Snug-fitting jeans and a trim tee shirt that emphasized well-formed muscles did nothing to keep heat from spreading into Ginny's cheeks. His welcoming smile reflected either forgiveness or forgetfulness of their cool parting at the museum. Ginny felt as if her inner musician played a longing tune.

Resisting the urge to drool like her dog, Ginny cleared her throat and tried to answer the professor in a coherent manner. "Uh, good afternoon, Professor Hallmark, you have a cute dog." She chose not to pursue the fact that he'd replied to her previous comment, which referred to the adorable Chihuahua not the cute man. Years of teaching had taught her that some things were best ignored. Now, if she could just convince her errant thoughts to not wander to the man, whose description tended toward handsome rather than cute.

"The name is Scott." Intense blue eyes studied Ginny as the professor reintroduced himself.

"Your dog is Scott?" Ginny teased as she tried to laugh off the tension bouncing in the air between them.

"No, he's Carlos, you can call me Scott." He offered his hand as a peace offering, which Ginny tentatively accepted. As their hands met, so did their eyes. The world around them seemed to pause for a beat. A tingle emanated from their touch and it took a few moments before Ginny broke their contact with a shaky reply.

"Sure... Scott... Carlos, let me introduce my hound, Jezebel." Ginny released Scott's hand and waved between the two dogs, formally introducing them as if they were people meeting for the first time. She hoped the introduction would draw attention to the dogs and away from her cheeks, which were probably growing redder by the minute.

Jezebel and Carlos rubbed noses, then Jezebel plopped to her side while Carlos continued his perusal.

Noticing the garden trowel and flower tray, Ginny asked, "How do you like your new surroundings?"

"This place is great. It reminds me of my grandparents' home. They always loved flowers. When I saw this house, I knew I had to have it. I'm putting in a few extra petunias this morning." His eyes sparkled with excitement as he viewed his home and gardens. "The most important thing about this place is that it's not far from the college, if I should ever need to walk there. In fact, I walked there and back this morning for a meeting about my theater camp for kids."

"I'm glad to hear you're interested in keeping the flowers going." Ginny fidgeted as she changed the subject away from theater. "I've always admired them on my walks and hoped that whoever purchased this place would keep up the gardens."

She smiled at the professor, deciding that maybe he might be all right. At least he would be if he could mind his own business concerning anything about the musical. Choosing to leave on a positive note, Ginny untangled her dog and bid the enticing professor farewell. At the edge of his yard, she turned for one last glimpse of Scott, bent over his flowerbed.

As he raised his head and gave her a dimpled grin, Ginny turned away with a smile of her own. A sudden longing to have both the flowering yard and its owner swept over Ginny, causing her to turn back once again for one last glance at the man who now stood waving at them. Briefly raising her own hand, she pivoted and pulled Jezebel around the corner, her mind full of confusing but pleasant thoughts.

Jezebel managed to trot away at a brisk pace, keeping up with Ginny's hurried exit. Good grief, she'd only met Dr. Scott Hallmark three brief times--make that four now. Her heart shouldn't be racing from the brief encounter in the man's front yard. Besides, she would not have freedom this summer for cultivating friendships. The musical would take up most of her time and she feared her show wouldn't stand up under the eyes of a professional like him. He might not even be a Christian, so she should put him out of her thoughts right now. Worse than that, he might destroy her dreams like James had done before.

As Ginny circled around the block toward home, she focused her thoughts on the musical and whispered earnest prayers. *Please Lord, give me courage. Give us the right words to say for the upcoming meetings. Let the enthusiasm generated at the first meeting continue as we reach out to each of the councils in the next few days. And Lord, help me with these feelings I have for the professor. Maybe he can just become a friend--one that will not interfere with my musical!*

❤ ❤ ❤

Scott stood with trowel in hand and watched until Ginny and Jezebel turned the corner. He smiled to himself as he thought of the glow that emanated from Ginny's cheeks. She might not be willing to admit it yet, but it looked like she might be as interested in him as he was in her. Not that he planned to do anything about it. Too many other commitments called his name. Carlos whimpered at his feet and Scott rubbed the Chihuahua's head before turning back to the flowerbed.

"Looks like we might both have a girl in our future, doesn't it, boy? Make that our distant future."

The little dog yapped and ran in circles. The long leash twisted around Scott's ankles, leaving them both tied in knots.

A ping from his phone interrupted his thoughts. His email notification flashed with the information that the musical's script had arrived. Reality slammed into Scott's chest. Could her passing visit a few minutes ago have been a plan to get on his good side? What a tangled mess. His thoughts wavered between trust and distrust as he leaned down to free his Chihuahua and his heart.

Falling for someone now would be more drama than this theater professor needed. At the moment, he had too much to untangle.

Yip, yip, even Carlos agreed.

Chapter 6

Five days later, June kicked off with lively chaos. Scott found himself in a tangled group of children who seemed determined to create a shipwreck of his summer camp. The events hadn't even started and already the children were running amok. Maybe a summer camp wasn't one of his more brilliant ideas. A little diva named Susanne twirled through the crowd, pretending to be a princess as her mother stood by, extolling her talented darling to another parent.

A bold little boy named Derrick added to the chaos as he cheered on her antics and created some mischief of his own. A few parents stood at the check-in table and didn't look too happy at the noisy din. Scott stepped away from the mass of children and sat down at the table to collect forms. He pasted a welcoming smile on his face.

"Sorry folks, I'm a little short on help this morning, but my grad assistant should be here any minute. I'm not sure what could be keeping him. Children, please find a seat and think about something you want to learn in camp." Scott sighed as half of the campers settled into small groups and the volume went down a few decibels.

Derrick mumbled something about wanting to have fun, not learn. Susanne continued to flit around the room. Scott quickly signed the waiting students into camp. When he had accounted for everyone, except a recently enrolled student named Melissa, he stood to take command of his new drama troupe. He needed to put an end to the chaos.

"Hey, kids. Let's show some respect." A feminine voice took the words right out of Scott's mouth.

"Miss Cline! Sorry, we're just excited." Derrick took the lead as other voices chimed in their apologies and the room settled into relative calm.

Disappointment filled Scott's thoughts as Ginny Cline and a tall man gently tugged a small girl into the room. So, she was married and had a child. He welcomed his last camper with a forced smile, fighting the sinking feeling in his chest. He should be relieved that she would not be competing with his goals for the year. The youngster must be the missing Melissa. Her last name wasn't Cline, but that didn't mean much these days.

"Hello, Professor Hallmark, I'd like you to meet Melissa, and this is her guardian, Lachlan Russell." Ginny's voice was all business as she made the introduction.

Mr. Russell shook Scott's hand as he patted the little girl's shoulder. "Thank you for this opportunity. We hope your camp will help our girl come out of her shell a little. My wife, Chelsea wanted to come this morning, but she had a last minute conflict. She will be picking Melissa up, so you can meet her later." Mr. Russell hugged Melissa, and then nudged her forward as he edged his way to the door.

"Hey, Melissa, come and sit by me." Susanne's voice rang above the chatter in the room as she waltzed her way over and took Melissa by the arm.

Scott waved his hand between Ginny and the youngster. "So you're not..."

"I came along for the moral support. I'm her teacher at school and suggested she might benefit from this experience. She's had a rough start in life, but things are so much better since the Russells became her foster parents."

"That's a relief," Scott said. Ginny shot him a questioning look. "Speaking of relief, I know we didn't get off to the best start the other day, but if you have time, I seem to be short an assistant. The kids respect you. Is there any way you can stay for a few minutes?"

"I take it you haven't worked with children before?"

"Only a few professionally trained kids..."

"Okay professor, maybe I can teach you something today." Ginny rounded up the kids with a musical greeting and introduced them to their new teacher. "This is Professor Hallmark, who will be leading your camp. Let's show him how well-behaved Forest Glen students can be."

Scott shook his head in awe as the kids obediently moved into a circle and began introducing themselves by acting out their favorite summer activity. The timid woman, who shook in her boots at the museum presentation, blossomed in front of his eyes as she worked her magic on the children. *Had her shaky performance at the museum been an act?*

Even shy Melissa joined in the fun. "This is my first summer here, so I want to do everything." She danced, jumped, and swam around the circle as Susanne clapped. Derrick gave her a fist bump when she returned to her spot between him and her cheering friend.

"How about you, Professor, what is your favorite summer activity?" Ginny asked.

Scott saw green as she flashed her emerald eyes at him and waited for his answer. He finally stuttered out, "I'm going to enjoy working with this great group of campers."

"Come on, Professor. We all acted out something silly. Now it's your turn." Derrick's cheeky grin dared Scott to do better.

"Well, when you put it that way, I should do something spectacular." Scott spread his arms wide and then transformed into an elephant. He stomped around the circle and waved his arm like a trunk. He stepped closer to Melissa and pulled a coin from behind her ear. "I enjoy going to the circus during the summer and now, I would like you all to pretend you are a performer in my circus."

Ginny cheered as his little circus grew. Susanne walked an invisible tightrope. Melissa tamed a wild lion named Derrick, while clowns and creative creatures pranced around ringmaster Scott.

"Great practice, everyone. Now, I want you to circle up again and each act will share what you've been working on." Scott looked around to find Ginny stepping out the door, which his tardy assistant now held open.

Pride filled his chest as he thought of what his new students had accomplished in the last few minutes. However, he groaned with regrets as the door slammed shut and a hungry lion roared nearby. He had to stop letting her affect him this way. He hardly knew the woman at all. Besides, he had a circus to run.

"All right, campers, are you ready for a really big show?"

♥ ♥ ♥

After a successful Monday night presentation for the City Council, Ginny spent the rest of June's first week hunched over her computer, adding dialogue and more tension to the script. The additions flowed easily when she realized that many of the scenes she had cut for brevity now helped expand both the plot and the deeper meaning of the musical. Good thing she'd saved those discarded scenes on her computer. During her brief time at the drama camp, she realized the need for including more children in the musical. Some of the songs and skits she had used for field trips and classroom teaching fell into the script as if they were ordained to be there. She clapped her hands and looked toward heaven.

Thank You, Lord, for bringing everything together at the right moment!

❤ ❤ ❤

Late on the following Sunday night, Jezebel started doing a nature call dance. Stars filled the dark sky when the anxious hound flew out the back door with a *woof*. Ginny stared up at the midnight moon and breathed a sigh of relief, knowing she had reached her revision goal. She should be tired, but energy surged through her body, giving her the strength to proofread for a few more hours after Jezebel came in and snarfed down a treat. At 2:00 AM, she finally decided to email copies to Annie and Kara for a final critique. She debated sending one to Melody, but decided she still wasn't ready to share everything with her musically trained friend.

❤ ❤ ❤

On Monday evening, Ginny nursed a big headache as she sat in the crowded county council room. Too bad this group had not been as cooperative as the drama campers were the first day of camp. Answering questions about unknown budgets and deadlines yet to be set up had taken a toll on her pounding temples. Her musical was in better shape, thanks to her revision writing spree, but her sleep-deprived brain wasn't computing budget numbers. Annie stood beside her and blustered her way through some of the trickier questions, but it would be a miracle if they got the matching grant they desired.

The council had stepped from the room for a discussion. The two women sat in cushioned seats, waiting for an answer.

"I'm not sure our presentation went as well as the ones at the museum and the city." Ginny fingered the chair's frayed arm rest and brushed her hand against the nap of the maroon velveteen covering.

"Don't doubt yourself." Annie's exuberant spirit flowed into her voice. "By the way, I heartily approve of what you've done with the script. The additional scenes with the children should bring in lots of parent ticket sales. I sent a copy on to Edmund this afternoon. This council should give us tons of support with all that you've done for the community."

When the solemn group of representatives returned to the room, none of them made eye contact. Ginny grabbed Annie's arm and held on as she prepared to hear the worst.

"At this time, we don't feel we have enough information to offer all of the money requested. Our proposal now stands for donating half the requested funds for the production of a community musical. Is there any discussion?"

Annie laid her hand over Ginny's and squeezed. They were not offering the hoped-for amount, but at least the County Council proposed something. They'd just have to seek other sources of financial aid.

During the discussion, one of the council members suggested that a more detailed list of expenditures would have made a difference in their decision. When they called for the vote, Ginny closed her eyes and prayed as the room filled with a chorus of "ayes."

"That makes it unanimous." Ginny and Annie gave each other a weak hug as the vote for the county's contribution to the musical became final. Support had passed City Council last week and now some funds were coming from the surrounding county. The donations from these two groups would provide much-needed startup resources for the musical. Even though the dollar amount didn't match the funds they had originally hoped for, joy radiated from one face to another as the two women accepted congratulations and encouragement.

Edmund Bradley bustled through the welcoming crowd and made it clear to everyone that he would lead the production team. "In fact, ladies, I think we should plan on having a committee formed soon. There are grants available for us if we can identify a steering committee and besides, it will help us keep things moving along."

Ginny nodded as she accepted congratulations from another council member. Excitement pulsed through her body as she shook each outstretched hand. Edmund's voice droned on. What had he just said?

"By the way, Ginny, can you speak at the June Business Men's breakfast? They've been known to donate money for projects like this one, and I have you tentatively booked for June 24th." Edmund's gaze met hers as she gulped and tried to find an answer.

Doubt churned in her stomach, but she nodded a reluctant acceptance. Would she be able handle something this big? Could she deal with all the committees? Heaven knew she had no understanding of budgets. The idea of more speaking engagements sent shivers down her back. Where would she find the time to do all that and still finish editing the musical? Bewilderment gurgled in the pit of her stomach. The tremor in her hands and heart spoke to being overwhelmed, but with God and Annie at her side, she would have to try.

As Ginny focused again on Edmund's conversation, she heard him ask about who might be on the committee beside Ginny, Annie, and himself. Should they have representatives from both the city and township councils?

Ginny's mind scrambled for someone to suggest and remembered the support her former room-mother had given at the museum. "Grace Cole from City Council might be good. I've worked with her on parent activities at school. She participates well and is a good leader. She also mentioned the possibility of getting support from the hospital auxiliary. What do you think, Annie?"

Annie added, "Great choice! Grace is influential in this town and I'm sure she will help us. I wonder if David Ericson would consider being our county representative. It looks like he already left the meeting tonight. Last week he seemed supportive after the presentation you gave at the museum. His skill as an advertiser could be a valuable asset for promoting the play. His wife, Kim writes a column in the *Gazette*, too."

"Now you're thinking, ladies! How about you contacting David, Annie--and Ginny, will you check with your friend, Grace? See if they can meet next week on Tuesday evening."

After agreeing on a time, Edmund bustled off and started chatting with several people from the council clustered in one corner of the paneled meeting room. The women saw their chance to exit and headed for Ginny's car.

Annie rubbed her hands together. "Maybe I should make Aunt Joy's blueberry muffins for the meeting next week. They're your favorite, aren't they, Ginny?"

"They are the best I've ever had. However, we better get busy making lists, like how many costumes and which props we'll need. I'll check my outline and adjust it a little. We'll definitely need a better budget before the presentation at the business breakfast in a few weeks. Things are happening so fast, I can hardly believe it, but I think our musical is going to succeed!"

Ginny's little car hummed to life as they settled in for the ride home.

"Didn't I tell you it would? This musical sells itself."

"You did, Annie, a million times over. I'm just sorry my presentation tonight wasn't enough."

"Now don't start doubting yourself again. They gave us plenty of ideas on how to make the next meeting successful, and that's what we're going to do."

"Just in case, do we have any plans for saving money?"

Annie answered, "I have at least ten dresses and a few dress patterns in the mansion's closet that represent the Pre-Civil War era."

"Would that green dress I used for the field trip last year work?" Ginny asked.

"It sure would. Aren't you friends with the woman who owns Miss Hope's Fabric Boutique?"

"I am. Maybe she'd give us a discount on cloth. I imagine the sewing circle at my church can help put costumes together."

Annie's eyes twinkled as she suggested, "Maybe you should ask your mother to help with the sewing. She has quite a talent with the needle."

"Mom does have a flair for costuming. That might be something to keep her occupied for a while. We'll have to limit her choices of patterns and fabric. Otherwise we might have to hide her zany outfits or put her costumes behind a big prop." Ginny chuckled as she remembered wearing some of her mom's creations to school during her elementary years. She put a stop to wearing those outfits after her first day in junior high. Mom's ruffled leopard skin jumper design provided too much fodder for the cliques that formed during those oppressive years.

"Speaking of props, we can look through the museum buildings for items we can use on the stage." Annie started naming baskets, blankets, kitchen utensils, and old chests as possibilities as they pulled into her driveway. "Come by the museum tomorrow and we'll do an inventory." She got out of the car and waved good-bye as Ginny pulled away.

Thoughts of the musical gave Ginny chills as she continued her drive home. There were so many things to do. It had been a nice distraction to concentrate on costumes instead of fretting during the drive to Annie's home. A little positive self-talk would keep her spirits going for a while. Though tonight's financial support did not fulfill every need, it supported a step in the right direction. *Take that to the bank, Mr. Doubting Professor...* A good plan for costumes and props had come together. God seemed to be opening the right doors. Thanking the Lord for the way everything had come together, Ginny turned on her car's media player and sang a praise song along with her favorite Christian artist.

♥ ♥ ♥

A week later, the aroma of warm blueberry muffins greeted Ginny as she entered the old mansion at the Forest Glen Historical Museum. She'd been there most days during the past week as the two women explored the village for props, but when Annie greeted her, the older woman bubbled with excitement.

"David Ericson finally returned my call and will be at today's meeting with his wife in tow."

Mrs. Ericson always kept her eyes open for something new to write about in the local paper. Ginny hoped the musical might be perfect for *Kim's Komments,* a well-read column in the *Forest Glen Gazette.* A favorable review by Kim could provide them with not only free advertisement, but might also draw in other financial supporters.

"Grace Cole is really excited to be on this committee, too. She said Mayor Kyle wants everything coming together as soon as possible. She hopes we'll be well-rehearsed and performance-ready for the Fall Fest," Ginny reported. Her mouth watered from the scents emanating from the kitchen.

Annie pulled a pan of fresh muffins from the oven and dropped them into a waiting basket. "I think David felt the same way. Have you thought about how soon the final revisions for the musical can be done?"

Before Ginny could answer, Grace arrived and began discussing the possibility of speaking to the hospital auxiliary. Soon

Kim and David Ericson joined them. Kim snapped Ginny and Annie's picture as they stood by the mansion's large fireplace.

Kim asked Ginny, "How did you come up with the idea for the musical? What is Annie's role in its historical background?"

Ginny relaxed with David and Kim and enjoyed telling the stories behind *Incident at Woodson House*. Her dreams about the musical became a reality through hard work, curiosity, and mutual information sharing with the dynamic Annie. The vivacious museum curator had pushed them to seek among the local political body for funds.

Now, it looked like the musical was on its way to becoming a reality, thanks to local support making the potential production so much nicer than either woman had originally hoped. Both Annie and Ginny felt overwhelmed by community backing for expanding and underwriting the musical, from a simple event at the Forest Glen Historical Museum to expanding into a large stage production.

"I just hope they don't expect me to build a stage here on the museum grounds." Annie teased the group as she pretended to hammer the top of her coffee maker. Laughing, she retrieved the carafe and filled cups for those who were now taking seats around the table, waiting for the rest of the group to join them.

Edmund Bradley strode into the committee meeting, more than a few minutes late, and announced in his authoritative voice, "Don't worry, Annie, I've got everything under control. I've got the perfect stage and a professional director on board."

Ginny masked her shock at the word *director*. Wasn't she going to be in charge of her precious script? If not her, then who, and where would her play be staged?

"The show will take place in the college theater and Scott Hallmark has tentatively agreed to join us as director. He can use his influence at the college and summer camp to encourage student actors of all ages to try out for this production."

"But where does that put our Ginny?" Annie voiced the question plaguing her friend.

"Why, she'll still be in charge of everything, since she is our little composer and author extraordinaire. We just thought it would be helpful if we had someone who has actually done a musical on stage before."

"We...?" Ginny forced the dismay from her voice.

"Yes, Scott and I... He didn't want to jump on board at first, but I encouraged him to think about it. I reminded him he has a perfect starting group with the summer camp I endowed."

Just what Ginny needed, a coerced director who she wasn't thrilled about having in the first place. How could this possibly work out in the long run? After meeting Scott and his dog, Ginny had formed some wishful thoughts about the professor, but having him unwillingly in charge of her musical made her want to stomp her feet. His lack of confidence with the campers had not given her a good impression about his ability to direct. Ginny let out a frustrated sigh.

"Don't you worry about a thing, young lady. With my backing, your creation is going to be fantastic. Scott really knows what he's doing, and his experience will ensure the musical is a success. Oh, speaking of our professor, he wants to know if you've found out anything about costumes yet. He has an idea for the set but doesn't want the backgrounds to clash or blend too much with costume colors or patterns."

"I hadn't thought costume colors would be an issue. I guess our uh--director may know what he's talking about," Ginny reluctantly conceded, knowing they really needed Edmund's financial support to make the musical a success. Conflicting emotions drummed their way into her thoughts. If the museum had not been at risk, could she walk out and forever give up her dream? That very moment? She gave the idea a fleeting thought before common sense and a spirit of strength overrode her irritation. She forced the rest of her response through unclenched teeth. "Miss Hope's Fabric Boutique can get our cloth at wholesale prices and The Needlers at First Church are willing seamstresses. I guess I'll check with Mr. Hallmark before we choose the material."

"That would be a wise idea. By the way, you should call him Dr. Hallmark or just Scott, which is what he is to everyone but his students."

"So, is Dr. Hallmark making his glorious presence known at our meeting today?" Ginny could not contain her sarcasm this time. Annie's quick kick under the table reminded her to harness her irritation. "Sorry."

"Don't worry. I'm sure you will someday look forward to his

'glorious presence,' as you put it. He will add professionalism to your little endeavor." Edmund adjusted his expensive tie and gave Ginny a look that brooked no argument.

This time Ginny contained her angst to a nervous leg shake, hidden under the tablecloth that covered the meeting table. Inside she boiled. Annie gave Ginny a gentle squeeze on her shoulder as she stood to retrieve her plate of muffins. Warmed by the friendly support, Ginny forced her negative thoughts aside.

"Excuse me, Edmund, would you care for one of my muffins? They're very good, and come from my Aunt Joy's old family recipe." Annie's interruption broke the tension crowding the room as Edmund reached for a warm muffin and began savoring its rich taste.

"Very delicious. You must share it with my cook--and to answer your earlier question, Ginny, the good professor will be joining us shortly. He stopped by his church first to meet with his worship band's leader. She and Scott are very close. He's hoping the little sweetheart can add some instrumental color to your arrangements and perk them up a bit."

Ginny's mouth sagged open in dismay. This could not be happening. They were changing her music? The man thought it needed perking up? The professor's little sweetheart would add some color to her arrangements! She didn't know what hurt worse: the fact they didn't think her music was good enough, or the information about a little sweetheart out there waiting to spend time with the professor as they worked on her project.

It shouldn't matter that the professor cared for another woman, but it still hurt for some reason Ginny refused to explore at the moment. At least he went to church. Maybe his church connections had shaped him into a decent human being. Hopefully, any Christian values in his life would reflect in his dealings with Ginny and the musical.

Notes from Beethoven's Fifth Symphony filled the air. Edmund pulled his phone from a pocket and began a conversation. "What? Really? We'll miss your input today but she's certainly more important at this point. Yes, I'll relay the information as soon as we're done. Bye." He put down his phone and turned to the others at the table.

"Sorry about that. Scott just called to let me know his lady friend is having some problems that need to be addressed right away. He has to stay and help her. The good news is, she agreed to help with the arrangements, and the praise band will provide live music for the performance as a donation. We won't need to look for an orchestra. He also wanted to let Ginny know he read the revised script you sent the other day, and thinks it has potential. He wants to start by discussing how to tweak the scene where the lead characters realize they are committed to each other and the proposal takes place."

Potential? That comment could be taken several ways. *Tweaking the proposal?* Ginny's heart fell. She'd spent the last few weeks revising, and the proposal scene in the final act pulled at her heart strings. Maybe Mr. Know-it-all could tweak it for himself if he thought he knew everything about romance. Perhaps he did, since there was some "little lady" out there.

Ginny hadn't had a date for the last year and a half, and at the moment wondered if she would ever start looking around for someone. If she found time after finishing the musical, she would cross the bossy professor off her list of possibilities. Her recent attempts at romance came from occasional library book checkouts from the inspirational romance section. Teaching duties during the day and grading papers at night left very little time for a social life. During college, James had made her well aware of her over-commitment to school. Ginny crossed her arms as disappointment wove a discordant tune around her heart.

Edmund patted Ginny's arm and tried to answer her concerns. "No worries. He said it came off more like a television scene rather than one for the large stage. It's just a matter of making the little things more obvious. He wondered if you could meet him on Thursday afternoon and go over his suggestions."

"I guess I can, but tell him to make it Friday. I have other plans for Thursday." Ginny gained satisfaction in knowing she could at least control the professor when it came to setting a time for a date. No--a meeting. She only felt minor guilt knowing her limited plans for Thursday included Jezebel's nail trimming and cleaning out the refrigerator. No power-hungry doctor of theater was going to rule her life, even if he did make her heart pound a rhythm here and there.

Annie's cleared throat drew Ginny's attention back on those

who were at the meeting. Thoughts quickly turned to fundraising, grants, and organizing the production team. One major expense would be costumes.

The group approved Miss Hope as head costumer, with the church ladies doing the sewing under her watchful eye. Ginny withheld the fact that her mother would be joining the group, as she assured the committee of the sewing circle's reputation. No doubt, there would be a few jazzy bows here and there, courtesy of Mom's unusual tastes. Annie would serve as an advisor to the sewing group by providing patterns and historical style suggestions. Flickers of excitement filled Ginny's chest as she imagined the colorful costumes.

"Don't forget, my director will have final say when it comes to colors used for the clothing." Edmund's comment doused the sparks ignited in her heart. Why had the professor given in to the man? He obviously did not support the musical.

David Ericson interrupted the building tension. "Once the director approves a set design, my brother and his construction crew will build the set at cost." His comment brightened Ginny's thoughts. At least someone had something positive to contribute.

David continued, "My advertising company will create a poster for promoting the musical. If we use the same design, we can also absorb most of the cost for printed programs."

Grace presented some good news, too. "My company has an empty hall that would be perfect for rehearsals. I also talked to Mayor Kyle's wife. She and her daughter, Rylee, have offered to supervise painting the sets."

"Excellent. I love the murals they did on some of the downtown businesses." Annie rubbed her hands together as her smile broadened.

Ginny's optimism grew as their plans fell into place. She allowed her frustrations over the professor to fade. Then Edmund passed her a note at the end of the meeting with Dr. Scott Hallmark's phone number. "Call him; you'll need to schedule your Friday meeting."

Chapter 7

"Well, that's a strange-looking orange. This fruit looks like it's growing a beard." Ginny tossed the offensive object into the trashcan. "Take that, you bearded piece of mold. I wonder how long you've been rotting in the crisper." She peered farther into the refrigerator and pulled out a disgusting lump of bagged food. "I'm in charge of this kitchen and it's time for you to go." She added the bag to the smelly pile of food. At least she had power over her messy refrigerator. Too bad she could not say the same about her precious musical. Beard or no beard, she wasn't going to let the professor or anyone else mess up her musical this time around. She hummed a song about having confidence, from one of her favorite musicals, while she continued her food hunt.

Baaow-woof? Jezebel pushed her nose in next to her owner's hand.

"No, you can't have any of these old scraps, Jezebel. I don't want to make another trip to the doggie emergency room for a tummy pumping, you silly beast." Ginny paused and scratched behind her dog's long ears.

Woof, woof, woof. Jezebel howled when a text message signal buzzed from Ginny's phone. *Will see u tomorrow. 1:00 at Sky's Place. Thx for the tip about using teen helpers at camp. I recruited 2 kids from my church,* appeared on the screen of her phone. It was about time Professor Scott got back to her. Too irritated to call him directly after the Tuesday meeting, Ginny had left a text message on his phone saying she couldn't meet on Thursday, but could do so at a local restaurant on Friday.

She'd offered the suggestion for camp as an effort to be kind. Even though he irritated her, she didn't want her kids from school to suffer at the camp. He hadn't bothered to get back to her until two days later. She resisted the urge to grind her teeth and laughed instead. Jezebel cocked her head and joined the fun with a muffled *woof.*

That know-it-all professor would certainly be in for an

interesting surprise at their meeting. Sky's Place served the spiciest chili in town. Maybe that would warm him up a little. Not that he needed much spice. Even Annie pointed out his good looks after everyone left the planning meeting. Ginny couldn't help but laugh as she remembered how her dramatic friend fluttered her eyelashes and put her hands over her heart when she talked about Scott's appearance. She informed Ginny that her married state did not make her immune to the drop-dead gorgeous man.

Jezebel's clicking paws on tile flooring took Ginny's mind off the handsome man and back to the reality that she needed get her beast ready for the nail appointment. The lazy, laid-back dog rarely objected to anything, except who she allowed to trim her nails. Unfortunately, Ginny did not make that list. After lugging the bag of spoiled food to the outside trashcan, she loaded her hound into the car. Then she headed off to Dawn's Doggie Dream House for Jezebel's monthly nail trim and pampering.

♥ ♥ ♥

"Hey, Dawn, are you ready for Jezebel?" Ginny entered the dog groomer's shop and released her hound.

"As ready as we'll ever be. Has she had any interesting misadventures since last month?" Dawn knelt and gave the top of Jezebel's head a rub with her knuckles.

"Well, she did try to eat a bee. You should have seen her chubby cheek afterwards." Ginny chuckled.

"It looks like she made a full recovery. Did you take a picture?" Dawn wrapped Jezebel's leash around her hand and stood up as Ginny pulled out her phone.

After sharing a good laugh over the picture of the bulging basset jowl, Dawn took the wiggly hound into the backroom to work her magic.

While Jezebel went in for her special treatment, Ginny visited the bookstore next door. She had missed reading her normal quota of books during the year it had taken to write *Incident at Woodson House*. Now that the writing process neared completion, she hoped to find more opportunities for light reading before rehearsals began in earnest. As she browsed through the bookstore's inspirational fiction section, she found the latest sequel in a series of books she had been reading over the last few years. Happy to find the book, she collected it and made her way to the checkout, where a familiar clerk waited.

"Hi, Ginny, would you mind if I don't put your purchase in a bag today? We're trying to be a little greener by not using too many plastic bags."

"No problem, Christy, I'll probably start reading it right away if Jezebel isn't done with her nails yet." Ginny gave the friendly clerk her debit card and waited for her receipt.

"How is that wacky dog of yours?" Christy smiled as she finished the transaction and tucked the receipt into the book.

"Nuttier every day, but I love her. See you later."

"Enjoy your book and give Jezebel my best." The clerk and Ginny shared a smile and waved good-bye to each other.

Ginny strolled down the sidewalk, and as she entered Dawn's Doggie Dream House, began inspecting the writeup on the back cover of her new book.

"*Looking for Love?*" Scott's familiar voice asked as he flashed his brilliant teeth.

"What?" Ginny's jaw dropped as she stared at the professor. Warmth filtered up her neck and into her cheeks.

"The name of your book--it's *Looking for Love*." Scott cleared his throat, drawing her attention to his well-formed Adam's apple. "So, what are you doing here?"

"Uhh--Jezebel is here for a nail trim." Was there anywhere she could go where she wouldn't run into this man? If he didn't embarrass her, he told her what to do or interfered with her life.

"At least I know you weren't avoiding me when you said you couldn't meet today." Scott smiled a knowing smile.

She wanted to sink through the floor from misinterpreting his comment about her book and the acknowledgement that she had used the dog appointment to avoid seeing him.

"So, is Carlos in for a little pampering?" Ginny attempted to turn the conversation from herself and the constant blush that betrayed her emotions.

"No, guys don't get pampered. He's just getting his nails clipped, too. He doesn't like it when I try to trim them. I tried cutting them a few times but decided I value my fingers. They come in handy when I'm playing piano or guitar." Scott ran his fingers over an invisible keyboard, then strummed an air guitar chord.

"Ah, a man of many talents, and ten fingers..." Ginny couldn't help but look down at the man's strong hands. Her mind strayed to the other day when he had held her hands a few seconds longer than necessary when she first met his dog, Carlos.

"More fingers to hang on to my dog's leash with. Hey, Carlos and I are going to go check out the trail that follows the old railroad tracks after we leave here. Edmund said I should check it out since the railway played an important part in the musical's history. Would you and Jezebel like to go with us?" Scott's offer seemed cordial, but she hesitated.

"I guess we could try. Jezebel has her limits when it comes to walking. Maybe she'll be inspired when she has Carlos to chase-- unless the little lady you were meeting the other day has any objections." Ginny felt comfortable with the suggestion of walking the dogs, more than if he had asked a more personal question or one that pertained to her precious musical. She couldn't resist reminding him of his relationship with another woman.

"I'm sure she would be fine with two friends walking their dogs together." Scott gave her a puppy dog look that seemed to beg her to accept the invitation.

"Hmmm, I'm working on that friendship part. Give me some time to think on that one, Director Hallmark." Ginny put one elbow in the palm of her hand and tapped a finger on her chin as she pretended to give the offer some thought. She couldn't believe she flirted with the man.

"Hey, remember, my name is Scott, and we can talk business tomorrow, not today. Let's go enjoy a nice summer afternoon with our dogs."

Woof, woof.

Yap, yap.

Both dogs appeared, led out by Dawn and her assistant. The animals wore matching bandanas and appeared eager to go on a merry chase down any trail they could find.

"That settles it." Ginny looped Jezebel's leash around her wrist.

"Great minds think alike," Scott agreed.

They both spoke at once, and taking their respective canines, headed toward the trail that ran behind the row of stores and out into the countryside. To Ginny's amazement, Jezebel trotted briskly along, trying to keep up with the wiry little Chihuahua. As they walked, Ginny and Scott occasionally bumped arms, sending her emotional well-being on a rising crescendo. Watching the breeze lift and blow his hair around in the gleaming summer sun proved more interesting with each step they took. Ginny furtively sneaked peeks in his direction, enjoying the show.

"Is everything okay? You seem a little distracted," Scott asked, when Ginny almost tripped over Jezebel, who had slowed to inspect a bug meandering across their path.

"Sorry, I've got a lot on my mind." *Including you and a certain lady I need to remember has an interest in you. I also need to get my mind off your looks and back on track for the musical.* "About the musical..."

"Remember, no business today. Just enjoy these pleasant summer days while we have them." Scott pointed down the trail and beckoned her to continue on their adventure. Maybe without the musical between them they could enjoy each other's company as friends for a while.

She nodded agreement, and they finished their walk in companionable silence, broken occasionally to point out interesting wild flowers and critters they spotted along the old trail. The sweet fragrance of honeysuckle emanated from wild bushes. Ginny couldn't resist stopping to pull the nectar through the flower and onto her waiting tongue. Scott laughed at her childlike enthusiasm and joined her merriment. Bright greens of summer lined their path as they traveled the old track bed and then reversed their steps back to the parking lot. After making final arrangements to meet at Sky's Place for their business meeting the next day, Ginny and Scott went their separate ways, with a lot to think about.

♥ ♥ ♥

Scott sat in his vehicle as he watched Ginny's car pull away. He'd enjoyed their walk but wondered why he'd even suggested it in the first place. Yeah, he had to develop a working relationship with the woman, but attraction was fighting against his doubts of being used. Attraction seemed to be winning the race as confusion churned in his gut. If he didn't get a handle on things, he'd get an ulcer for sure. Wouldn't that be a great thing to have when he met her at the chili place tomorrow? He'd need some antacid for sure.

♥ ♥ ♥

"So how's your chili? Is it spicy enough for your taste?" Ginny couldn't help but feel a little satisfaction as she noted Scott's cheeks turn a deeper shade of pink after his first few spoonfuls of the renowned chili.

"It's definitely got a zing to it that I haven't tasted before. I'm still trying to figure out what spices are in this concoction. It doesn't taste like any chili I've ever had and there's a certain aftertaste I'm trying to figure out." Scott cleared his throat as his face took on a brighter hue. Reaching for his glass of water, he downed half its contents to counteract the effect of the unidentified spices.

"Don't try to figure out what's in the chili; the secret recipe's been handed down for generations. No one outside the family has been able to decipher it yet. Just enjoy the unique taste, and next time try some spaghetti and cheese with it. Your taste buds will appreciate the difference." Ginny pushed a bowl of oyster crackers his way and indicated they might help curb the effects of the hot chili.

"Speaking of secret recipes, do you think your friend Annie would be willing to share her chocolate iced brownie recipe with me?" Scott took another deep gulp of his drink and cleared his throat again.

"You're a cook?" Ginny couldn't help but smile as the professor dealt with the spicy chili. Watching him proved more interesting as she tried to imagine the man in a chef's hat. She couldn't picture him in a kitchen, no matter how hard she tried.

"No, I'm not really much of a cook, but my lady friend, who's helping us with the musical arrangements, heard about them and would really like to try making some herself." Scott held a napkin to his mouth and muffled a burp. "Pardon me." He looked at Ginny in a way that expressed pride in the other woman's cooking ability.

Ginny shouldn't have, but she felt a wave of disappointment at the subject of the mysterious female. Facing her reaction, she plastered a confident smile on her face and asked, "So does this lady have a name?"

"She's never told me her real name. She said it was an embarrassingly old fashioned one, so I just call the adorable little lady Honey."

"How sweet of you." Ginny hoped her comment didn't come out sounding too snarky, but from the puzzled look on Scott's face she wondered if he understood her confused feelings. Hopefully she hadn't embarrassed herself too much.

"Speaking of honeys, you've got one honey of a dog. I'm just trying to understand how you came up with the name of Jezebel."

Ginny leaned back in her chair, happy to change the subject. "I adopted her from a basset hound rescue society. They said she had a reputation for ruining things. I named her after the evil queen in the Bible who seemed bent on destruction. She's earned her name from her past and a few misadventures since I've had her. My hound has a thing for eating Bibles and sandals. I guess you could say she likes to feed upon the Word, since I've lost a couple of leather-bound Bibles and my favorite pair of sandals to Jezebel's appetite."

"Ah, the lady has a sense of humor. Speaking of which, I really liked some of the lighthearted moments you included in the musical."

"But you didn't like my proposal scene." Ginny couldn't help but express her disappointment.

"It has possibilities, but will need some adjusting when you put it in a theater before a live audience. When Honey and I read through your script the other day, we both agreed there were elements perfect for television or in a movie production that won't go over as well on stage."

"So Honey's an expert in musicals?" Ginny tried to hide her growing jealousy of the unknown perfect woman who kept popping up in their discussion.

"She's had some stage experience, but that's irrelevant at this point. When she read the leading lady's role and I did the other part, it just didn't come together the way it should."

Ginny bit her tongue, trying to keep from saying something she would later regret. In addition to defending her manuscript came the knowledge that she needed to halt whatever feelings she had for Scott. Controlling her emotions for the good of the play and out of respect for his relationship with Honey was the right thing to do. She had enough trouble waffling between attraction and dislike for the professor. Ginny turned her focus to the musical and asked about his suggestions.

Scott pulled his laptop from its bag and brought up the script Ginny had emailed him, after getting proofreading corrections from her friends. With heads bent together, they perused the scene in question, with Scott pointing out what he thought needed to be changed.

"From this day on, I'm going to support your cause with all my heart. I want to work by your side as a loving husband. What do you think, my lady?"

Warmth coursed through Ginny as Scott read the proposal line and looked directly at her, as if expecting an answer. "I, ah, I don't see what's wrong with the line. It sounds like the perfect proposal to me." She crossed her arms and stared at him while she fought to keep her eyes from filling with tears. Why did he want to kill off her darling scene?

Scott briefly met her gaze before tapping the computer screen. "His words seem a little stiff and unnatural, but that's an easy fix. In addition, you need to change the staging directions here. The couple needs to move to the apron at the front of the stage. If you have them in front of the curtain for the proposal, it will allow for a backdrop change before the next scene."

Ginny nodded as she tried to accept his suggestions. Most of the adjustments made sense, but an internal battle raged in her belly. She didn't want to make any changes to her precious script. However, the suggested wording had sounded better coming from his lips.

Scott's suggestions continued. "Instead of offering her a tiny ring, the hero could offer his intended a family heirloom locket, which would be placed around her neck and easily seen from the audience as she accepted her lover's proposal. Here, let me demonstrate."

He took a college ring from his hand and slid it onto her finger. A passing server raised her eyebrows but kept walking. Then he placed a hand on his neck and lifted off his college ID lanyard. "Will you take this pledge of my love, dear lady?" He stood and draped it over her neck as restaurant customers broke out in a cheer. "Can you see how that got everyone's attention?"

Ginny lifted the lanyard from her neck as heat coursed up her face. "You've made your point about this prop substitution. I understand now why you wanted to alter a few things, but I need some time to think before we make any major changes to the dialogue."

She pulled the laptop closer and added the staging notes. When she dared to look up from the computer, she noticed Scott's cheeks had taken on a ruddy color. The tint accented his rugged complexion and made his reddish hair seem to glow even brighter. Maybe he wasn't as immune to what was going on as she thought. Very appealing, but stealing someone else's man didn't fit her values, even if she couldn't help but notice his appearance. Maybe the red in his face was just the full effect of the chili finally kicking in.

She needed to stop letting her mind wander. She pushed away quickly from Scott and the table where the computer sat. She waved down the server to get their bills and began searching her purse for some singles to use for a tip. Her hand stilled as Scott gently laid his warm palm over her wrist.

"No need for that, this meal is on me. It's been my pleasure to dine and work with you today." His eyes searched hers for agreement before he gathered up both bills from where the server had laid them and reached for his wallet.

"Thank you, for the meal and for making *Incident at Woodson House* better. I'm sorry for thinking your ideas wouldn't work. I think I understand now." She paused and shouldered her purse before daring to look into his blue eyes again.

Scott slid their chairs under the table. "Speaking of ideas, could we meet some place on Monday afternoon and go over plans for set design? I have several thoughts on what might work, but I'm getting the idea that you would probably like to have input on what we choose."

"That would be correct, professor. I definitely want to be in on most of the major decisions since this play is so close to my heart. Could we meet at the museum around two? It's open this Monday and Annie wouldn't have a problem with us using the kitchen table to spread things out on."

"Would we be distracted by museum visitors?" Scott's warm look sent messages she refused to interpret.

"They aren't supposed to come in the kitchen area since it's used mainly as a place for volunteers to get their coffee and enjoy a treat from Annie's home kitchen."

"Annie's cooking! Her treats would be a definite distraction, but a very appealing one at that. Sounds like a plan, but could we make it 2:30? I have camp in the morning and then Honey needs a ride to the dentist. I can't guarantee I'll be back by 2:00."

Honey again... "Sure, that would be fine." Ginny couldn't

keep the disappointment out of her voice, but she forced a smile and waved good-bye to the professor.

❤ ❤ ❤

On Monday, Scott offered Honey his arm as they left the office building. Thankfully, his graduate assistant and the teens had volunteered to handle cleanup after the morning camp, allowing Scott to get the lovely lady to her appointment on time. Now if he could just keep things moving along to make his later meeting with another lovely woman.

"Watch your step, Honey, there's a big hole in the sidewalk. Let me help you get into the car so you won't twist your foot on the cracked cement."

"Don't mollycoddle me, Professor Hallmark. I may be over seventy, but that doesn't mean you have to treat me like an old lady." Honey put her hands on her hips and glared mockingly at him.

"I'm only trying to be a gentleman. At least let me get the door for you."

She nodded her acceptance and slid into her seat as Scott acted the part of a gallant. After closing the door, he hurried around to the driver's side while she snapped her seatbelt in place.

"How was the dentist appointment?"

"It went well. The few teeth I still have are doing fine, thank you, and the new dentures are clicking along nicely. I told him I didn't want any of those fancy implants. They cost too much money for a young independent woman like me. Thank you for taking me here today."

"No problem." Scott turned the key and put the car in gear.

"Fred called from the garage and says the old jalopy will be as good as new by Friday, so if you're available then, could you take me out there in the afternoon?"

"I should be able to, unless I get too tangled up with Miss Ginny Cline." Scott couldn't help but smile at the mention of the longhaired beauty.

"Ah yes, your new lady friend, the writer and composer extraordinaire. Is she pretty? Is she your new honey?"

"Almost as pretty as you, my fine friend, but you are the only one I call Honey, at least for now. Maybe someday I'll think about a relationship, when I'm not bogged down with camp or the musical, or trying to ensure I have a permanent position at the college."

"So there might be hope for you yet, young man." Honey's gaze seemed to probe Scott's face for evidence of his interest in Ginny.

"I'm not sure. When I'm around her, I'm a little confused about whether she's interested in me or not. One minute I think she is and then all of a sudden it's as if she can't wait to get away from me."

"Very interesting… So how did she take to the suggestions we came up with the other day? I hope she liked them."

"At first she resisted, but after we put our heads together, she understood most of what needed to be done to make everything better." Scott turned his head away from Honey as they sat at a stop light. He pulled at his collar and adjusted his seatbelt, which seemed tighter than usual. He knew she would draw her own conclusion if his face had turned red.

"So you put your heads together, did you? How close?" Honey's teasing let him know she noticed his discomfort.

"Close enough to smell her sweet lavender shampoo."

"And what do you know about lavender shampoo?" Honey laughed as more warmth coursed up Scott's neck and into his face.

"Well, it sure smelled like the bottle I picked up for you last week when you couldn't make it to the store because of your broken down jalopy. Thank goodness they put the shampoo in a separate bag from your prescription or it would have leaked all over your medicine."

"What can I say, the girl has good taste when it comes to shampoo. Let's hope she has as good taste when it comes to choosing a fine fellow like you."

"Hey, we've only met a few times. Don't rush things. I have no idea how she really feels about me, even if I do find her to be a very special person. Besides, you know I have to make it through this year before I can put down permanent roots at the college. So, when is the next time the church band is getting together to work on the songs for the musical?"

"Are you trying to change the subject, young man?"

"Possibly. Is it working?"

"Not on your life. Now tell me more about your young lady."

By the time Scott got Honey situated in her cozy cottage on the far side of town, he was running about fifteen minutes behind schedule. He sped across Forest Glen to the museum's mansion, hoping there were no police officers on patrol. Not finding Ginny in the kitchen when he arrived, he wandered through the old mansion until he heard voices coming from the basement stairs. A blast of musty air swept up from below as Scott bent over, avoiding the low-hanging ceiling over the stairs. He followed the melodic sound of their voices until he discovered Annie and Ginny in a small room. They faced away from him as they sorted through a rack of ancient clothing.

"What do you think of this one, Ginny? I have a dress pattern that is a similar style and it would fit the era the musical is set in."

"I like it. I hope Scott does too. Unfortunately, I'm sure he'll want input on the colors we choose. I can see ways that we could change the style a little by adding different aprons, collars, or trim. Those little touches would make each dress different in its own way while preserving the style of that era."

"So it's Scott now. You must have decided the professor is okay to work with after all, or could there possibly be more to using his first name than just business?" Annie's shoulder bumped her friend in a teasing manner.

"I'm able to work with him for now. He seems to know what he's doing, but there are some complications making it harder for there to be anything more." Ginny's voice sounded sad as she continued in a muted voice Scott could barely understand.

Realizing he was eavesdropping, he conquered his curiosity about her reasons for not being interested in him and took a step back toward the basement entrance. He called their names loudly as he re-entered.

"Hi, Annie and Ginny, sorry I'm late. Honey's appointment took a little longer than I expected."

"Is she okay?" Annie inquired as she pulled several dresses from the rack.

"She had a routine dentist's visit, so I think she'll do just fine. Her car's been out of commission for a while, so I volunteered to take her in. Hey, are those some dress styles that fit the historical period for the musical? What can you tell me about them?"

♥ ♥ ♥

Ginny studied the professor as Annie went into detail about

waistlines, puffed sleeves, and accessories. Her first impressions of a bossy know-it-all faded as Scott took in Annie's information with great interest and attention to detail. His bright blue eyes lit with excitement when Annie shared the information that Miss Hope would be able to get reproduction fabrics in a variety of pastel colors.

Scott rubbed his chin. "The musical will require more outfits than what's hanging here. I hope you have a crew of seamstresses who are willing to put more costumes together."

Ginny put her hands on her hips and answered, "The Needlers from First Church are ready to sew as many dresses, pants, and shirts as we need. They are a talented group of women."

"Don't forget the special petticoats your mom will be creating," Annie said.

"What will be special about them?" Scott asked.

"Trust me, you don't want to know. Just be glad her buttons and bows will be well hidden beneath several layers of cloth." Ginny winked at the museum curator and could not help grinning.

"Here, Scott, try on this coat." When Annie helped him don the ancient waistcoat, Ginny noticed his sandy curls brushing against the back of the coat's collar. As he modeled the long coat, Scott looked ready for a wedding. Ginny turned away and reminded herself of his devotion to Honey.

"These are all great, and I think if we stick with a variety of pastel colors for the ladies and natural colors for the men, everything should work with the sketches I have for possible sets." Scott shrugged out of the coat and placed it back on a hanger.

"Are you an artist too?" Ginny couldn't help wondering what talent the man would come up with next. Instead of being Mr. Know-it-all, now he'd probably prove himself Mr. Perfect. She didn't know whether to be intrigued or irritated.

"I can only dream of having that kind of talent. My claim to fame in that area is having a membership on a website that designs sets and backdrops. Most of these have easy construction plans that someone could build or rent at a reasonable cost. The stage manager at the college took a look at these layouts and is more than willing to work on the set design and building team, along with David's brother." Scott flashed a winning smile at Ginny, making her forget about Honey, the set design, and building crews. Maybe he was Mr. Perfect after all.

A quick elbow jab and knowing grin from Annie brought Ginny back to reality as the threesome left the basement and headed up the stairs to lay out the scenery designs on the mansion's dining room table. Ginny almost giggled at her star-struck admiration of Scott, hoping he hadn't noticed. However, Annie wasn't the only one grinning as they made their way to the kitchen.

❤ ❤ ❤

Scott smiled to himself as he acknowledged there might be a chance Ginny cared for him. Honey would be so happy for him when he told her about what had just happened. If he hadn't imagined it, he thought he heard Ginny sigh as she stood there staring at him. Now, if he could just figure out why she ran hot and cold when he was around. Maybe Honey could give him a clue about the woman's behavior. He'd ask her opinion when they set up for tonight's praise band rehearsal.

❤ ❤ ❤

"You don't have a clue about what she's thinking, do you?" Honey made her way through the church door as Scott held it open.

He leaned against the doorframe and frowned at the elderly woman. "No, that's why I'm asking you. One minute I think Ginny is giving me mooneyes, and the next she's laughing or running away from me in disgust. I just don't get it."

"Well I can tell you this, young man, she is interested in you if she's giving you mooneyes, as you call them, but something or someone is holding her back. You haven't said anything to offend her, have you?" She shook a finger at his chest and bent her head back to look him in the eye.

Scott grabbed her finger and wrapped her arm around his elbow as they walked toward the church office. "Our conversations have mostly centered on advice about the play, but she seems fine with that--most of the time. She really fell in love with the mock-ups of the set that I took to the museum the other day, but when I asked her if she wanted to go out for coffee, she turned me down flat. It was almost as if I asked her to betray someone."

"Maybe she already has a boyfriend," Honey teased, as she turned on the copy machine and held out her hands for the packet of music Scott carried under his arm.

"I haven't seen or heard any evidence of a boyfriend." He

crossed his arms, knowing he sounded a little defensive.

"Maybe she's not a coffee drinker." She winked at Scott as she slipped the songs into the copier.

"Hmmm, I don't think I've ever seen her drink coffee. I'll have to try a different approach next time."

"Why don't you invite Ginny to something at church? Isn't your Bible study group going out for pizza and fellowship some Friday?" Honey shuffled completed copies into bundles and clipped them together with paper clips.

"Now, that's an idea. I found out she goes to First Church, a sister congregation to ours, so maybe that would be a good approach. Thanks for the idea."

"Anytime, sweetie, now let's get busy arranging this music. It looks like your girl provided a decent piano score with guitar chords for all the songs. The praise band should be able to jump right in and add some stylistic touches to the songs without any problem." Honey shoved the copied packets of music back into his hands and headed for the sanctuary.

"I like the sound of that. I could get used to thinking of Ginny as my girl." Scott whistled as he stepped on the stage and offered Honey a hand up.

"Come on, son; get your mind on the music. You're starting to sound like a teenager. The band's going to be here any minute and we need to spread this material out before they get here." She had the audacity to giggle as she placed the copied packets on music stands.

Right on cue, the band began to straggle in and tune up their various instruments. Amid twangs, strums, and thumping drums, Scott visited with the band members and told them details about the play and events in the scenes supported by the songs.

"Several of the songs will naturally feel better if we play them like an old-time band from the time period, but there are a few more dramatic pieces requiring a romantic ballad or pop song style. Listen while I play the first piece on the keyboard, and then let me know what you think." Scott's fingers nimbly ran through the song, bringing it to life with his skillful touch as Honey's strong but aging voice sang through the touching lyrics.

"Wow, you'd never know that song came from an amateur composer," Claire, one of the band members, commented as others nodded their agreement. "The words really touched my soul."

"It may be a song about slaves seeking freedom," the lead guitarist said, "but we could use it on a Sunday morning to speak to the hearts of people who need to find freedom from their sins and problems in this world. Do you think the composer would allow us the opportunity to sing the piece for our church?"

Scott agreed the song was inspiring and promised to ask for permission to use the piece in a worship service. "If I can talk her into letting us use the song soon, it would be good publicity for both the musical and the auditions that will take place after the Fourth of July."

"The band doesn't have to audition, do we?" Don, the drummer, tapped a rim shot on his snare drum and then brushed the cymbals.

"No, but you're going to have to do a lot of extra practicing with Honey, and Ellen will have to man the keyboard since I will have my hands full being the director. I hope we can get the sweet little composer over here soon to hear how you're progressing."

"So she's sweet, is she?" Don couldn't resist teasing Scott.

"Is she sweeter than Honey?" Claire joined in with the good-natured jabs.

Ellen gave Honey a gentle squeeze. "Watch out, Sugar, you're going to lose your sweetheart to a younger woman." Everyone knew of Scott's openhearted generosity in helping the older woman during her recent time of need.

"It's about time the professor loosened up a bit and found himself a younger woman." Honey continued the ribbing the other band members had begun. "I've only known him for a few months, but I think our 'sweet little composer' Ginny just may be the one that God has planned for good old, I mean young, Professor Scott."

"Thanks a lot for letting the world know," Scott said. "Don't get your hopes up too soon, everyone. She hasn't even agreed to go on a date with me yet."

"Have you asked her out already?"

"Did you forget to brush your teeth or something worse?"

The teasing continued as the band practiced the inspirational music. Ginny's well-prepared manuscripts proved easy to play and soon extra flourishes and trills embellished the music, through Honey's knowledgeable advice or by band members making their own decisions.

As Scott sat back to absorb the music, his mind drifted to the image of the composer's long, wavy brown tresses. As he daydreamed about running his fingers through her brown hair, a portion of his distrustful heart opened to new possibilities. He began to think of ways to convince her he was more than the unwelcome director of her play. Perhaps something would come up after the production ended. He knew he should take things slowly. After all, he had to succeed at his new job with the college and prove worthy of their tenure track. He'd learned from past experience that women had no interest in a man without a steady job.

Chapter 8

"What am I going to do with you, Jezebel? I can't believe what you did this time, and it's not funny. I should be heading to Miss Hope's shop right now. Instead, I'm dragging my circus clown dog down the street." Ginny did her best to remain angry at her strange-looking pet. Jezebel smirked a goofy dog grin and woofed a hearty bark as she wiggled her strawberry stained and spotted body. A whiff of strawberries floated into Ginny's nose as she trailed behind her dog.

At least the neighbors had been willing to forgive the wrinkly dog's trespass into their strawberry patch. However, their hilarious laughs over Jezebel's new looks were more than a little discouraging as Ginny thought of toiling over the bathtub in search of a clean animal. Hopefully, no one else would spot her polka dotted dog before she reached home.

"Now that's something I've never seen before: a pink spotted dog."

Ginny stopped in her tracks. She couldn't believe Scott had chosen that moment to take a walk down her street.

"Are they offering a new service at Dawn's? I don't think Carlos would be interested. It might insult his masculinity." Scott chuckled at the sight of the strawberry speckled hound as Jezebel jerked on her owner's arm and strutted down the street toward home.

Ginny laughed along with Scott as she related Jezebel's latest misadventure in a nearby yard. In addition to eating a few berries, Jezebel managed to roll around in the patch and cover her body in lovely fuchsia spots. Having to get the dog clean and secured at home would delay her Wednesday afternoon outing to Miss Hope's Fabric Boutique.

"There's a big tub in my backyard that the former owner must have used for cleaning vegetables. I'm on my way home from camp, so why don't we just keep going until we get to my house? Then you can scrub her off in the tub." Scott grinned when Ginny easily agreed to his suggestion. As they walked up the street, several neighbors passed them and either looked curiously at the dog or asked directly about what had happened. Carlos' yapping barks from the front window welcomed them as they arrived at Scott's house. Minutes later, both Carlos and Jezebel were splashing in the tub of sudsy water. Shaking doggie bodies soon covered both owners in suds of their own.

"Don't look now, but I think Frosty the Soap Man is sitting on top of your head." Scott reached to knock the pile of bubbles off Ginny's hair.

A tingle trickled down from her scalp to her heart. Ginny's surprise changed to wonder as a look of brief longing passed between them. Then she shook herself back to reality. She needed to know where Honey stood in the equation before she let her feelings show. Grabbing a handful of lather, she heaped it on Scott's head with a nervous laugh and ran quickly away before he had time to react. Turning the hose on her dog, she rinsed the still speckled hound as best she could and toweled her down. Thanking Scott for his help, she made her excuses, saying she should head for Miss Hope's to see the fabric, which had arrived that morning.

"Then I definitely need to go with you." Scott's puppy dog expression put the basset to shame. "Take Jezebel home and I'll stop and pick you up after I change out of these wet clothes."

"But..." Ginny tried to think of a good excuse but couldn't seem to piece her thoughts together.

"No buts--besides, I haven't been to the fabric store. You can introduce me to Miss Hope, in case I would ever need to go on my own. Give me your address and I'll be there in a few minutes."

Numbly, Ginny nodded, supplied her address, and dragged the reluctant hound back to her house, where she pushed the dog into the confines of her laundry room prison. There would be no more adventures that day for the troublesome beast. Ginny quickly changed into dry slacks and a printed top, pondering what adventure lay ahead for her.

Nervously waiting for Scott to arrive, Ginny wondered why she'd accepted his offer to drive. She truly felt an attraction. At the same time, she chided herself for not finding out more about his relationship with Honey before agreeing to go anywhere with him. Rationalizing that the trip was business-related, Ginny pulled her emotions together and mentally prepared herself to remain on an even keel during the visit to the fabric store.

❤ ❤ ❤

Scott whistled a tune from the show as he jumped into his toffee-colored mini-SUV and headed toward Ginny's house. After their fabric shop visit, he planned to ask her out for a meal. Pulling up to her quaint little cottage, he noted her love of flowers. A bed of purple iris stood in the middle of the front yard, and a strip of wildflowers edged the walkway running from her porch to the driveway. There in the midst of that walkway stood his lovely flower of a lady, bending over to snap a wilted blossom from its stalk. Despite his hesitation about getting involved with anyone at this point, he wanted to call her his own. He just had to figure out what held her back.

Not that he was in a rush himself. He'd finished the first meeting with his review committee late on Tuesday afternoon. After that, he'd crashed at home for the rest of the evening, poring over documents he needed to file before getting on the tenure track. Heading to the fabric store provided the perfect excuse to avoid his paperwork and spend time with something, make that *someone*, more interesting.

"Hey there, sweet lady, are you ready for your chariot ride?" Scott rounded the vehicle and opened the passenger door with a flourish and bow.

Blushing prettily, the object of his affection smiled briefly and then shuttered her face as she retrieved her bag from the porch. She stiffly entered the car and huddled close to the passenger door. Puzzled, Scott observed her as he walked in front of his car and noticed a look of sudden determination cross Ginny's face. When he sat down and buckled his seat belt, he heard her clear her throat as if she were gaining courage to say something important.

After giving brief directions to the fabric store, Ginny asked, "So do you think Honey cares that you're spending so much time with me?"

"Oh, she's excited about this whole project and is really glad we're working together. She's even been teasing me about everything we've been doing. She's got high hopes for us."

"I have high hopes for the musical too, but I need to know if Honey has a problem with you calling me pretty. If I were her, I'm not sure I would understand why you're calling another woman pretty. By the way, turn left at the next corner and you'll see Miss Hope's shop."

"Are you saying that Honey might be jealous of me admiring your good looks?" Scott couldn't stop the laughter that burst from his mouth.

"I don't see what's so funny." Ginny crossed her arms and looked out the window as they pulled into the strip mall parking lot.

Stifling his laughter, Scott smiled to himself and then gently answered, "Sorry for laughing. I think you will have to meet Honey in person to understand that she would have no problem knowing how much I admire you. You are a beautiful person, both inside and out, and you are so talented to have written this outstanding musical. I admit, at first I doubted an amateur could create a musical like yours, but you have proven me wrong. Honey and I both love your songs."

Ginny nodded but gave no other response.

"Speaking of meeting Honey, the band practiced some of your songs Monday night and we were wondering about performing the freedom song during a worship service. If you're willing, we could sing *Freedom*, and I would love to have you as my guest at our church that day. What do you say?"

"Wow, I guess it would be great advertisement for the musical!"

"Exactly what we thought, especially Honey. She said we could recruit a few actors from our church by using the exposure of the song to our advantage."

"You're sure Honey wouldn't be bothered that I'd be your guest that day?"

"On the contrary, she will be thrilled to see you there. Like I said, I think meeting the dear lady will clear up a lot of things for you. I'll take that as a yes, as soon as we can work out a date. Now let's go in and check out the fabric before Miss Hope calls and reports some loiterers in her parking lot."

Ginny popped out of her door before Scott made his way around the vehicle--so much for trying to be a gentleman. He followed her retreating figure across the parking lot. For now, he could only hope for a minimal friendship if she kept running hot and cold every time he mentioned Honey. *She needs to accept that there will be changes to the music and the script of this venture. Honey can be her friend if she stops over-reacting when she hears her name.* For the sake of the musical, he needed to get over his heartfelt reactions to the woman and focus on developing a business relationship. It looked like Miss Hope's shop might be the perfect place to start working on that connection.

"Welcome, welcome folks," Miss Hope's mahogany cheeks glowed as they stepped through the door. "Is this the professor you told me about, Ginny? He's as handsome as you said, sweetheart."

Ginny furtively shook her head while Scott suppressed his laughter. He reached out and shook Miss Hope's welcoming hand. Plastic beads hanging from her braids clicked together as the jolly woman leaned in to give the surprised man a warm hug. Then she waved them both toward her workroom where the shipment of historical fabrics awaited their approval.

Artistic creations hanging on the walls immediately drew Scott's attention when he entered the back room. Fabric, ribbons, buttons, and rickrack had been skillfully sewn together to depict different scenes from around the town of Forest Glen.

"These are amazing!" Scott stood in awe as he surveyed the artwork.

"They're only a few of Miss Hope's creations. Most of them are down at the city museum." Ginny beamed at her humble friend, who merely smiled and waved off the compliment while she opened the packages of calico, gingham, and cotton print reproduction fabrics stacked on her cutting table.

Still gazing at the quilted creations hanging on the wall, Scott became aware of the women's whispered conversation and laughter. Turning their direction, he was stunned to see Ginny holding up a green print against her shoulder, which brought out the astonishing emerald of her eyes.

"Amazing." Scott couldn't be sure whether he said the word aloud or to himself as he stared into her beautiful eyes.

"I believe you made that comment already, so how about getting over here and checking out the material Miss Hope picked out for us to use in the musical?" Ginny's annoyed comment snapped Scott back to reality.

"Uh…right. You should wear something in that green shade,

Ginny, it really brings out the color in your eyes."

"Actually, I may consider auditioning for a small role in the play since someone else has been given the director's position." Ginny's voice reflected mild resentment.

"Ouch, I guess I deserved that. So do you think you would be willing to try out for the lead?"

This time it was Hope who hooted in laughter. "You should hear her warble."

"I *have* heard her singing but I'd like to hear more of her warbling, as you call it," Scott coaxed.

"I warble best when I have my favorite singing partner, Miss Hope. We sometimes do duets at our church for special occasions." Laughing together the two women smiled at each other and broke out into a two-part rendition of *The Old Rugged Cross.* Ginny's clear soprano voice blended easily with Hope's resonant alto to create a touching harmony.

"I must be the luckiest director in the world. I haven't even had a first round of auditions and may have already found my two leading ladies."

"Look here, Mister, I may not be the director, but I still have a major interest in *Incident at Woodson House.* You will pick the best singer for the lead role, which isn't going to be me. I have an aversion to performing for large crowds. After all the presentations I've done lately, I think I might be ready to handle a small role. Though, the more I think about it, I think my friend Hope should definitely audition, don't you?"

Scott agreed, but bit his tongue so he wasn't tempted to say, "Yes, dear," in answer to her demands. The woman had certainly come out of her shell in the last week. He had no doubt she could conquer her fear of crowds, based on his recent observations. Chuckling to himself at the thought of being her henpecked husband, he began earnestly looking at the fabric and discussing the possible choices of costumes for each character.

"So how come someone like you hasn't found yourself a sweet little wife by now?" Miss Hope asked the question Ginny hadn't dared broach.

Scott answered, "It's really hard to have time for much of anything outside of school and theater when you're working toward a doctorate in the business. If I wasn't doing school-related assignments, I filled my spare moments trying to earn enough money to pay for my schooling or doing internships at local theaters to gain experience. Now that's all behind me and I'm hoping to settle down in this town for the long haul."

"So how long have you known Honey?" Ginny interrupted.

"I moved here this spring and she greeted me the first day I went to church with my new boss. She's just one of those people you fall in love with from the moment you meet them." Scott paused as he reflected on meeting the engaging woman who reminded him of his favorite grandmother.

"How nice," Ginny replied in a flat-toned voice.

"Just wait, you'll fall in love with her too, Ginny." Scott smiled and looked at her with hope in his eyes.

"If you say so--now, what do you think would be a good color for the runaway woman's dress?" Ginny held out two bolts of material and looked relieved to change the subject.

"How about this one?" Scott held a bolt of cloth near Hope's face. "This really brings out the color of her eyes, don't you think?"

"I'm beginning to feel a little coerced here, but you know what, for the sake of my good friend Ginny, I might try out for the role. Did you know that my grandfather said one of our ancestors came out of slavery using the Underground Railroad?" Hope picked up the cloth and nodded to confirm her decision to give the musical a chance. "I'll do it for the sake of my friend Ginny and my heritage."

"Hope, I had no idea you were related to someone who traveled on the Underground Railroad, and we've been friends for such a long time. I could have used you for a resource when I did my research," Ginny said.

"That's all right. All I have is oral family tradition. No one kept any written proof back then, and if they did, they didn't share during those days. That way none of the conductors on the railroad would have been caught, back in the day. Local historians were lucky when the Woodson descendants discovered evidence in that hidden room during their renovations."

"They were lucky and I've been blessed to use that information for the musical."

Scott shared information on auditions with Miss Hope and she readily agreed to come on the condition that Ginny would sing with her. She got into the spirit of the moment, and soon they were helping her shred pieces of cloth, which they dipped in coffee from her handy urn. Hope then made plans to piece the cloth into a rag-tag skirt that would become her costume, if she ended up in that role in *Incident at Woodson House.*

A rush of late afternoon shoppers brought their meeting to an end. Miss Hope left to assist her lone employee cutting fabric and ringing up sales. Scott's rumbling stomach announced that the time for an evening meal fast approached. That gave him the cue he needed to ask Ginny if she would share some food with him.

"I see there's a sandwich shop next door. Would you care to join me for a quick repast?" Scott enunciated the request in a British accent and tipped an imaginary hat to Ginny.

"Why, kind sir, I do believe I hear your stomach rumbling. I guess it would be rude of me to deprive you in your time of need." Ginny continued the impromptu British acting.

Scott gratefully accepted her agreement. Ginny looped her hand through his offered elbow and they properly headed down the sidewalk until they reached the door to the eatery.

"After you, my lady." Scott made a slight bow.

"Thank you, you are such a gentleman." Making a quick curtsy, Ginny then entered the little sandwich shop.

"My mother trained me well, and by the way, this is my treat, so get whatever you want--another thing my mother taught me about treating a lady right."

"You're sure Honey won't mind?"

"Positive. You'll understand why when you meet her. Is this weekend too soon? The band's meeting again tomorrow night and I think we could put your freedom song together by Sunday." Scott waited expectantly for Ginny's answer.

"That should work since it isn't my turn to be a greeter at church."

"Great, then maybe the following Sunday, I can hear you and Miss Hope sing for your congregation."

"Will you invite Honey to come with you to hear us?"

"We'll have to see if she's available. Honey's a key member of the praise band, so it's a little harder for her to get away."

Ginny's expression changed as she turned and entered the line to order her sandwich. Every time Honey's name came up in the conversation, she zipped her lips and wouldn't look his way. What was wrong with the woman? She barely spoke as they made their way through the line, only opening up her mouth long enough to choose condiments for her sandwich. After completing her order for a baked chicken sub with most of the trimmings, she waited silently at the end of the serving line while the workers assembled Scott's roast beef sandwich. His mouth watered as the aroma of freshly toasted bread and warm meat swirled over the counter.

Once they were seated, Scott offered a blessing for their meal and the conversation turned to the weather and other mundane things. As they wrapped up their meal, Scott reconfirmed Ginny's commitment of coming to church with him on Sunday. Thrilled to finally have her definite agreement, he felt like jumping in the air and kicking his heels like he had seen Fred Astaire do in the old movie he watched at Honey's home last weekend. Maybe Ginny could be his Ginger Rogers. Come to think of it, Ginny and Ginger did have similar names. When they returned to his vehicle, he couldn't help but ask the question.

"So is Ginny your real name or is it short for something like Ginger, as in Ginger Rogers?"

"Only in my dreams--I like to watch Ginger and Fred's old musicals, but unfortunately I have two left feet when it comes to dancing. Virginia is my real name. Actually, my full name is Misty Virginia. My mother is a bit eccentric and my absentee father didn't care what she named her daughter, or my brother Nathan, either."

"Sorry your father didn't care, but I think your name sounds very lyrical, like the title of a musical. Honey and I like the old musicals too. Maybe we can pop some corn and make a night of it some time." Scott slowed for a stop sign and glanced her way before continuing toward her home.

"Won't three be a crowd? I think I'd be in the way."

"Are you kidding? Honey's looking forward to having you over and she's got one of the best collections of musicals that I've ever seen."

"Sounds like you've been over at her place a lot." She crossed her arms.

"We've been working together, almost every evening since we started prepping your musical. Though, I must say your arrangements haven't taken too much adjusting for our band to work with them. Honey and I both agree that they're downright astounding for an amateur."

"Thanks, I think." Ginny laughed.

Scott realized his expression probably passed from horror, to apology, to a bumbling look displaying his attempt to cover his messy reaction.

"No hard feelings. The arrangements were a true labor of love. The process for creating the accompaniments proved much more difficult and painstaking than composing the original melodies. Those tunes came to my mind as if they flowed straight from the hand of God. I sometimes wonder how they turned out as good as they did. I still have to pinch myself every once in a while when I think of how the musical came together."

Relief flooded Scott as he quickly put the car in park, jumped from his seat, and opened the door for Ginny when they arrived at her driveway. "I'll pick you up at nine Sunday morning. Our church is pretty casual, so no need to get too fancy." He brushed her hand in parting and both of them stilled for a few moments-- blue eyes meeting green--until Ginny cleared her throat, breaking the connection, and began searching for her keys. After one last good-bye, Scott made his way back to the mini-SUV, humming the *Hallelujah Chorus* to himself as thoughts of Sunday morning began forming in his head.

Chapter 9

Scott said casual. But, how casual? Ginny's thoughts tumbled over each other as she pushed through her closet, trying to decide between several different styles of slacks and skirts, to go with the striped top she had finally settled on. Opting for a long flowing skirt and a simple pair of flat sandals, she felt she would fit in no matter what level of dress was the norm for Scott's church. Now, she just needed to prepare her mind to meet Honey, who seemed to intrigue Scott so much.

He didn't seem to understand the idea that Honey might not appreciate the time he spent with Ginny. She'd found herself growing much too fond of interacting with the man. The hands on the clock approached nine, so Ginny quickly gave her hair one last brush, leaving it hanging free and long for her morning of worship. One last look in the hallway mirror revealed a confident-looking young woman who appeared ready to conquer the world, or at least one who had the Lord on her side.

Tucking a reluctant Jezebel into the laundry room, Ginny closed up the house and then sat on her porch to wait for Scott to arrive. Breathing in the fresh morning air and raising a silent prayer of praise helped focus her mind on the coming worship experience.

When Scott's car rounded the corner, Ginny left her comfortable white rocker and waved as she descended the gray wooden steps. He pulled into the drive and made his way around the car to open her door. What a kind gentleman. Rarely did anyone open doors for her, with the exception of an over-eager child performing door duty at school. She hoped Honey realized what a blessing she had in Scott.

"You look like one happy lady today." Scott welcomed Ginny as he helped her into his mini-SUV.

"I always do on Sunday. It's my favorite day of the week, in case you haven't guessed already. I love singing worship songs and it's always been a tradition in our family to do something special on Sundays."

"So are you doing something with your family today?"

"Eight o'clock tonight is Facetime on the Internet, or phones. My brother Nathan and I are heading over to Mom's so she can be in on the conversation. Jessie Cline is known for her arts, not technology. We're talking to some of our cousins who are scattered all over the United States. How about your family? Do you ever hear from them?" Ginny's dulcet tones revealed her love of family.

Scott smiled. "My parents, George and Courtney, call me every few days or so. Since I moved to this town, it puts me about an hour from home, so I do get to see them occasionally. In fact, I'll be traveling there for the Fourth of July weekend. My brother, Robert is planning on being there, too."

"That's a good thing for you. Mom is only about fifteen minutes away. Being nearby has come in handy a few times when Jezebel needed to get to the vet and it wasn't convenient for me to be off from school. It's nice to have someone around that you can rely on."

"Speaking of families, I hope you'll like my church family. They're a great group of people, especially Honey. She's such a sweetheart."

Ginny turned to look out the window as they approached the church parking lot, hoping to hide her reaction to the mention of Honey's name. Searching for something to talk about beside the woman, she commented on the rocks framing the entranceway to the church. "Such beautiful stones! They seem to sparkle in the sunlight."

"The way I understand it, early settlers actually harvested those rocks from the creek that runs along the back of the church property. Those stones became part of the original structure that stood on this site many years ago. When the congregation outgrew the smaller building, they incorporated the old stones into the entranceway of the new worship center. Maybe that's why the nickname for our congregation is The Church of the Rock, kind of a double meaning for the building stones and Christ the cornerstone. Come on, let's hurry. It's almost time for the service to start."

As they entered the sanctuary, a sweet-faced, dark-haired beauty sat at the keyboard playing a thoughtful prelude, setting the stage for meaningful worship. Members of the band standing by for the song service consisted of several men of various ages, a grandmotherly woman who surprisingly held an electric bass, and a beautiful red-haired woman in her mid-twenties. Ginny wondered whether the infamous Honey was the vibrant redhead or the gorgeous raven-haired woman. As the worship service began, she concentrated on the words of the songs and did her best to not think of the man at her side, and the two lovely women who were pouring their hearts into their praises.

When the song service ended, Scott excused himself to introduce *Freedom*. Ginny felt the loss of his presence immediately, but his warm voice drew her attention as he told the congregation about their project, the band's involvement, and then extended an invitation to the auditions.

"Today we are privileged to present a very special song to you. As the band practiced it this week, we couldn't help but see a great message for every person seeking freedom that only God can provide. We hope you will enjoy it and understand its message for your life. We are very privileged to have the author and composer with us today. Please welcome Ginny Cline."

Giving a quick wave and tremulous smile to the congregation, Ginny stood momentarily and then sank back down into the shelter of her padded seat. She lifted her gaze after a brief applause and focused on enjoying the first public rendition of her song. Amazed that Scott stayed on stage and picked up an unused guitar, she felt goosebumps raise on her arm as the lyrics of the song reached out and touched the hearts of the congregation. She had never realized the impact the song could have in a setting other than the musical. The arrangement Honey and the band had put together added to the powerful meaning in a very effective way. Very few dry eyes remained as the final chord died away and people sat in thoughtful silence. Ginny wiped a stray tear and bowed her head in prayer for those who needed God's love and freedom from sin.

Reverently moving to the pulpit, the white-haired and bearded minister gently broke the silence by thanking Ginny for giving them so much to think about through the song's words.

"When Honey asked me to bring a sermon today about freedom from sin, I had no idea how much the message of this song would impact us all. I don't think I can top what we've just heard, so bear with my humble additions and apply what you heard to your own life. Jesus is our only hope for freedom from all our worries, cares, sins..."

When the service ended, well-wishers and those deeply touched by *Freedom's* lyrics overwhelmed Ginny with words of thanks and praise. Hugs and handshakes alike accompanied invitations for her return to the warm-hearted church. As the crowd slowly thinned out, she eventually made her way to the stage where Scott, who had joined the band for the last song, stood talking to the instrumentalists on the stage. As if sensing her presence, he turned, stepped from the stage and put his arm around her shoulder in welcome.

"Hey everyone, I'd like you to personally meet my friend Ginny. Ginny, this is Ellen on the piano and Honey's over there on the bass..." Scott continued his introductions, but Ginny doubted she would remember any of their names if someone asked later. The sweet little old lady who had skillfully played the bass was the mysterious Honey. She'd been jealous of the grandmotherly woman who shared a friendly smile and waved, as she placed her instrument in its case. Ginny stood in stunned amazement and then burst into laughter.

"Hey, I know Drummond is a funny name for a drummer, but I've never had that kind of reaction before." The drummer joined in her laughter, which soon infected the whole group, and everyone enjoyed a good smile.

Ginny sighed in relief that the real reason for her laughter had not been obvious and reached out to shake hands with each of the band members. When she reached Honey, she couldn't help but draw the older woman into a close hug.

"I'm so glad to finally meet you. Scott has mentioned so many wonderful things about you and now I can see why. Your arrangement of *Freedom* is beautiful. Hearing the full accompaniment for the first time sent chills down my arms."

"Thank you, sweetie, Scott's said some pretty nice things about you, too. I'm hoping you can come over to my place this afternoon. I've invited the whole band for a potluck dinner. After that we'll come back here so you can hear the arrangements we've done for your other songs as well." The grandmotherly lady put one arm around Scott and the other around Ginny. Leaning close to Ginny's ear, she whispered, "Was it my imagination or were you relieved to find out that I wasn't Ellen or Claire?"

Ginny mustered a weak smile in answer. The realization that the stunning redhead must be Claire released a flood of hesitation from her mind. At least she would be able to remember the names of the other women. Hopefully they weren't as perceptive as Honey, who grinned from ear to ear as she pushed Scott and Ginny closer together and took her position behind them as they walked out the exit door.

❤ ❤ ❤

When Scott and Ginny got into his car, he reached for Ginny's hand, which she willingly gave for once. He was pleasantly surprised and wondered what had changed in the last hour. She seemed pleased with the song, but there also appeared to be something different as she smiled warmly in his direction. Had a wall fallen down or a door suddenly opened between the two of them? Whatever the case, he would not complain because he welcomed having her willing hand in his.

"Did you enjoy everything this morning?"

"Yes, I did--especially meeting Honey. She's much older than I pictured her from your descriptions."

"She has more energy than a lot of people half her age, so I guess I just never mentioned her being older. It's not like you had any reason to be jealous of her." Looking at their joined hands, the truth suddenly dawned on Scott. "You were jealous! You thought she was my girlfriend or something." He couldn't help but chuckle at the thought and Ginny withdrew her hand, crossing her arms firmly across her chest.

"I don't see what is so funny, Scott. You kept raving about all of her talents and missed our organizational meeting to take care of your 'little lady.' What was I supposed to think--especially when you talked about going to her house to watch old movies together?"

"Sorry, I didn't mean to laugh at you. The whole situation just struck me as funny. I guess I've been pretty dense about not realizing you thought Honey could be anything other than a friend. You did ask if she would mind the three of us doing something together. I guess I should have gotten a clue then."

"My point exactly..." Ginny's face glowed as she slowly gave Scott a forgiving smile.

"So can we start again? Let me introduce myself. I'm a single guy that moved to town not too long ago. I think you're pretty and a very sweet person. I have a great older friend, who reminds me of my grandmother. She would love for us to come to her house for dinner today so we can fulfill your dreams of creating a musical that will touch the hearts of the people of this town. Are you willing to forgive me for not properly introducing you to Honey from the beginning and join us for a meal today?" He gave her a pleading look before starting the car.

"I suppose I can--for the sake of the musical and the treasure of new friends in this venture of ours." This time Ginny reached over to take Scott's hand, after he maneuvered the car out of the church parking lot and headed towards Honey's house. "Do we need to pick up something for the potluck dinner?"

"No, Honey and I have that covered. I gave her money to get chicken from the grocery deli for my contribution. I also sent her your friend's recipe for brownies the other day and bought her the ingredients. She said she would do the cooking on my behalf for today, so we're all set."

❤ ❤ ❤

Throughout the meal, Ginny enjoyed making the acquaintance of Ellen and Claire, who were both happily married to other members of the band. Ellen shared the news that she had recently learned there would be a new little one added to her family around Valentine's Day.

"If our child is a girl, Don wants to call her Cadence, since she'll be the newest little drummer in the Drummond family." Ellen laughed as the proud drummer entered the ladies' circle, long enough to give his beaming wife a quick hug, before returning to the guys who were getting the latest baseball scores from the television.

Honey passed through both rooms with the plate of brownies and then settled down between Ginny and Claire on a worn floral sofa. "So Ginny, what do you think of our talented professor?"

Finding herself the center of attention, Ginny glanced toward the other room, where the men were loudly commenting on the ballgame. Realizing the men were occupied, Ginny quietly answered. "He is proving to be a very knowledgeable director for the musical." Disappointed looks from the circle of feminine faces encouraged Ginny to say more. "I hate to admit it, but I'm just coming to terms with any interest I might have in him. I thought he had a girlfriend until I met Honey this morning."

"You thought Honey was his girlfriend!" Claire exclaimed.

"You've got to be kidding." Ellen shook her head in disbelief.

"I like him a lot, but he's a little too young for me, sweetie." Honey added with a chuckle, "I wondered what was up this morning, until I started to figure a few things out. Trust me, Ginny, when I say you have my blessing to explore a relationship with Scott. While I love him like a son or grandson, I can assure you that he isn't interested in me that way. In fact, he's been telling me a lot of nice things about you."

"Oh--this sounds interesting," Claire crowed.

A sudden silence emanated from the other room.

"Is there something we should know, ladies?" Scott called from the other room.

"Definitely, but we're not telling," Honey retorted with a laugh. "I think the men should be on clean up duty today. The ladies are going to ride with me to church in the jalopy and set up for today's practice."

"Watch out, ladies, I hear Honey's quite protective of her old jalopy, so be careful." Don's voice carried over the baseball cheers in the other room.

Expecting to find an old beater, Ginny was surprised to be climbing into the backseat of a fiery red 1964 Mustang convertible in pristine condition. Twisting her hair into a braid and leaning back on it, Ginny enjoyed the short ride to church as Honey skillfully spun through the roads between her home and the place of worship.

"This is quite a car, Honey. How long have you had it?"

"Let's just say it's been a one-owner car and leave it at that. My electric bass and this car are almost the same age. They were both gifts my parents gave me for my college graduation, and then I hit the road trying to make it big in show business until I met my Mr. Right. We had a good thirty years before my sweetheart passed away from cancer."

"Were there any children?" Ginny asked, thinking that surely this loving woman had enjoyed bringing up children of her own.

"Unfortunately, we were never blessed with our own children, but I've had many unofficial adoptees, including your professor, who considered me their mom or grandmother over the years."

"I don't know if he's my professor yet, but I can tell that he certainly must love you--like a grandparent."

Ginny and the other women laughed at her pause.

"Let's make that *like a parent*. I've decided I'm not that ancient yet." Honey joined in the laughter and wheeled into a parking space near the church's entrance.

By the time the ladies had turned on all the electric equipment needed for the band, the men joined them and began checking tuning and arranging their music on the stands. Ginny sat back in wonder as she listened to the small but talented group bring her music to life. Adding her voice to the harmonies created by the band affirmed her desire to try out for a small role in the musical. As the songs were sung, she frequently found her gaze wandering to Scott and wondering how she would feel if he were to play a role opposite her in *Incident at Woodson House*. The gorgeous smile he frequently flashed in her direction added to her growing interest. As the afternoon progressed, her heart turned to thoughts of other dreams that might one day come true for her and Scott.

When the rehearsal drew to a close, Ginny received more than one invitation to join the group for their next Saturday evening pizza outing. Don and Ellen offered to pick up Ginny and Scott for a double date to the restaurant and Ginny gave in as she looked forward to fellowshipping with her new friends and the professor, who grew more and more interesting. The thought of a real date eased its way into a part of her heart that she'd protected for a long time.

Chapter 10

Ruffles of white netting filled the workroom in the back of Miss Hope's store. Ginny stretched her back and surveyed a row of sewing machines surrounded by white material. She'd joined The Needlers and spent a long Monday afternoon assembling undergarments for the musical. They would need more, once auditions provided specific people's measurements, but laughter had filled the room as the crew of women completed their first sewing project. She smiled at her mom, Jessie, who remained to help organize the chaos.

Hope moved around the room, modeling a fluffy petticoat. "I feel like a princess ready for a ball."

"If you want to be a princess then you better grab one of my fully decorated models." Jessie held out a skirt bedecked with bows and a small embroidered ruby-colored rose near the waistline.

"Maybe that one should be saved for your daughter's costume, or perhaps a wedding." Hope took her petticoat off and hung it from a hanger on a nearby dress rack.

"What's this, daughter?"

"Nothing you need to worry about, Mom. I have a pizza outing with a Bible study group," Ginny said.

"And a handsome professor as your escort..." Hope snickered and pulled another petticoat over a hanger.

"Hey, I barely know the man. Yes, I agreed to a date, but I have no idea if I can trust the guy. He could turn out to be another James, or even worse, someone like my father." Ginny's arms crossed as her mother hugged her close.

"I'm sorry things didn't work out between your father and me. Business took priority over family. I didn't exactly fit the mold of a corporate wife. I tried, but never seemed good enough. When his morals took a sharp turn for the worse, I took you away from that situation. I thought we had moved on after his death."

"I thought so too, Mom, but forgiving and forgetting seem to be two separate issues for me. Whenever I consider dating someone, fear of the past gets in the way."

Hope added her embrace to their circle. "Sounds like you need some serious praying, friend. Do you mind if I lift my voice for you?"

"Thank you; I definitely need your prayers."

"And maybe you need to talk about your fears with me or your mom, too."

After surrounding her with prayer, the three women sat and talked well into the night.

"Mom, how did you ever get over my father? He pushed us to the side without even caring."

"It wasn't easy. I had to lean on the Lord, even though your dad and some Christians rejected me because of the way I dress or act sometimes."

Hope and Ginny nodded with understanding.

"I think people thought he provided us with a living when we actually received nothing but bills. The good Lord knew how to take care of us, though." She fingered the ruby rose embroidered on the petticoat she held. Few people knew that the rarely recognized illustrator of educational books known as Ruby Rose, Jessie Cline to her family, had managed to make a living that secretly supported her family of two children.

"So how did you find the courage to start dating Roy?" Ginny reached for her mom's hand.

"I had to choose forgiveness over fear and let go of the past. I still pray daily for strength and wisdom. I'm also moving slow and Roy has been patient and accepting of the real me." She laughed as she added, "Old age moments are coming in handy by helping me forget the past, too. Now, tell me about this professor of yours."

♥ ♥ ♥

"Hey Ginny, tell me what's going on? I haven't heard from you in a few days." Annie's excited voice rang over the telephone airways. "*Kim's Komments* has us featured this week and the *Gazette* included a short article about our auditions in the Arts section of the paper. They must have interviewed the professor because the audition article mentions some of his experience. Did you know he did some acting in Chicago and New York? You may have to give in and recognize our professor's abilities."

"That's great news about the articles. Sorry I haven't talked to you lately, but I've been getting to know Scott better over the last few days."

"Oh, really...?" Her voice rang with happy curiosity. "Tell me more."

Ginny shared her adventures from the last few days, including the information about the mysterious Honey being an older but energetic woman who charmed the professor with her musical talent and love of life. Annie laughed and commiserated as Ginny told of her conflicting emotions and the relief that swept over her when she finally met the lovely woman, who truly was a honey.

"So do you think there's a chance you could fall in love with Scott, since you are using his first name?" Annie quizzed her friend, while Ginny smiled into the phone.

"I think there could be a possibility now that the confusion over Honey is cleared up, but I'm in no hurry about rushing into something as serious as love and marriage."

"So now we're talking marriage," she jokingly accused.

"We'll see. Did I tell you I'm thinking about trying out for a small role, since it looks like I won't be directing?"

"How fun... You'll be like Alfred Hitchcock who always made an appearance in his movies."

"But I won't be as scary as good old Alfred. I'm into happy endings like the one I wrote for the musical."

"Who knows, maybe your happy ending will be you walking down the aisle beside your professor." Annie could not stop encouraging Ginny's growing interest in Scott.

"He's not mine yet, so please don't tease him when we have our next meeting. We need to keep those business meetings on track for the sake of the show."

"Speaking of business meetings, do you need anything for your presentation tomorrow downtown? Edmund Bradley asked me to cater a dessert cart for the meeting, so I'll be there."

"That would be great. I can always use your input if I forget anything. Oh, and would you mind bringing a woman and a man's costume from the museum? I can use them to talk about the need to raise funds for the clothing."

"Great idea. I'll see you tomorrow, bye."

Wroof! Wroof! The basset hound alarm went off when Ginny shut down her cell phone. *Yap, yap* came an answering sound from outside as the doorbell rang, announcing visitors for both the ladies of the home. Quickly adjusting the barrette holding her hair back in a summer ponytail, Ginny greeted Scott and Carlos while Jezebel bounced at her side.

"Can we gents interest you ladies in an evening walk around the neighborhood?" Scott doffed an imaginary hat and bowed at the waist.

Jezebel made her choice clear by running faster than she normally did for her halter and leash when she heard the word "walk."

"It looks like the decision has already been made. Just give me a minute to get my walking shoes on." Ginny motioned for Scott and Carlos to have a seat on her flowered couch and went to the laundry room where her shoes had been left sitting after a backyard adventure with the basset earlier in the day.

Returning to her front room, Ginny couldn't help but laugh at the masculine man sitting on her very feminine couch, holding the tiny dog on his lap. Carlos gave Scott kisses on his cheek and wiggled with delight at the thought of walking with the girls.

"So, who's the boss, you or Carlos?"

"Oh, definitely Carlos--he rules at our house. Would you believe me if I said he had the idea for taking a walk with you ladies?"

"I might, but I think it would be a disappointment knowing you were forced into walking with us." Ginny faked a slight pout as she slipped on her shoes.

"Trust me, he didn't have to twist any arms. If Carlos hadn't thought of it, I would have come on my own. Are you ready to go?" Scott stood and moved toward the door, following the peppy little Chihuahua.

"Ready when you are. Hold on, Jezebel, give me a chance to close up." Twisting the lock into place, Ginny shut the door as she battled the basset who strained at the end of her leash. Joining Scott on the sidewalk, Ginny and Jezebel walked parallel to the man and his dog as they made their way toward a small city park.

They followed a sloping trail into the ravine that made up the park. Ginny revealed that the creek meandering through the bottomlands had probably served as a path for runaway slaves traveling through the area. Touching his arm to point out a trail that ran up to the Woodson House, she felt a sudden jolt of electricity travel through her arm and paused in her description of the path. Scott must have felt the connection too, because he turned toward her and offered her his open palm. Returning his smile, Ginny accepted his hand. The couple walked their happy dogs up the hill to view the old home that once served as a station on the Underground Railroad.

"Every time I take this path, I'm amazed to think that so many people came this way before me. All their hopes and dreams of freedom were reliant upon the next family on the Underground Railroad. It would be scary to put that much trust in someone you didn't know at all."

Scott pulled Carlos to a stop and turned to face Ginny. "Speaking of trust, are you starting to trust me?" Hopeful blue eyes searched her face.

"I believe so. Just, please allow me some input before you change anything about the script. It's been my dream for so long that every word and note has a special meaning to me."

"I'm not talking about the play. I'm thinking of something a little more…"

Jezebel howled and Carlos yapped as a chipmunk ran across the path a few yards ahead of where they stood. Ginny found herself dragged after her howling banshee, who chased the tiny woodland creature. They left a gaping Scott standing tangled in Carlos' leash. By the time both dogs settled down, the magic of the moment had passed, and the conversation turned to the upcoming auditions.

"Since you'll be trying out for a role and also helping with the auditions, it would probably be good for you to come a little early and do your singing and acting before we open the doors to the rest of the crowd," Scott said.

"Do you think there will be a big group of people looking to take part in the musical?" Her anticipation grew at the thought of the musical becoming a reality.

"Definitely. Most of the kids and teens doing the summer workshop with me are thinking of coming. The paper's done a nice job of advertising and I've had many inquiries from adults through email and phone calls as a result. Some of the other college staff and students may be interested as well, since we've been putting it in the campus newsletter this summer."

"That's great! *Incident at Woodson House* is really coming together faster than I thought it would when Annie and I first started a year ago."

"Speaking of the musical coming together, it would be really nice if we could get a recording of the songs for people to practice with once we have assigned their roles. Would you like to help the band put that together the next time they meet?"

"I'd be glad to. I really like the members of your band, especially Honey."

"Now that you know she's not my honey, right?" he said.

"Okay, I admit it, I did start to get a little jealous of your sweet little honey, so don't rub it in, if you know what's good for you."

"Speaking of what's good for you, why don't we swing by the Creamery and get a few scoops of ice cream? I've heard they even have a special doggie cone for Carlos and Jezebel."

"Jezebel loves going there and they have my favorite, butter pecan. I guess that makes it a date."

"Let's make it an official date, my lady." Scott clicked his heels and bent his head over Ginny's hand.

Drawing her other hand to her chest, she smiled and replied, "Sure, but first tell me your favorite flavor of ice cream so I can get to know you better."

"It's anything with peanut butter cups in it. I'm glad you're interested in getting to know me better because that's what I would really like us to do." He reached out and rejoined their hands. "By the way, are we still on for going to your church this Sunday?"

"That's the plan. Hope and I have been practicing a new song she heard on the radio a while back. It has a positive message about putting the Lord first in your life. We do need to get there early, though. I didn't kid you when I said I served as a greeter. Our church is small, so my turn comes up pretty often."

Arriving at the ice cream parlor, they made their order from an outside window and sat down to enjoy their treats at a wrought iron table set in the shade of one of the trees lining the street. Jezebel wolfed down her treat in a matter of seconds. Carlos slowly licked at his doggie cone and it soon became obvious that he needed to defend himself from the drooling hound. Ginny and Scott had their hands full containing the ambitious basset. When Carlos had filled himself to the point of bloating, they released the hungry hound, who pounced on the leftovers with glee.

As the well-satisfied dogs waddled their way home, their owners followed them with joined hands and hearts open to exploring their blossoming interest in each other.

Stopping at Ginny's door, Scott brought her hand to his lips and lightly kissed it. The old-fashioned gesture stirred her heart in a sweet way as they parted for the night.

Leaning against the inside of her door, Ginny hugged herself and let her mind wander to the man who walked down her sidewalk. She'd only known him for a few short weeks and already he'd gone from someone she resented to a person with lots of possibilities. Such an interesting and talented man--who knew what the future might bring? Her heart seemed open to learning more about Scott Hallmark. She only hoped he would prove to be a better man than James or her father. She pushed that thought away with a prayer, thinking of her recent conversation with Hope and her mom.

Ruff, ruff. Jezebel interrupted her train of thought by dragging Ginny to the back door. Ice cream had a way of working quickly through the dog's system and nature suddenly called to the hound.

♥ ♥ ♥

The next morning dawned bright and early as Ginny and Annie entered the restaurant where the breakfast for the businessmen's association met. Annie laughingly pointed out that several of the 'businessmen' in attendance were business women and wondered if they realized the need for a name change.

"I don't care what name they use as long as they give us some support for the musical," Ginny answered as they set up the display of costumes Annie had provided for the presentation.

"Long time, no see." Scott's cheery voice rang out from behind the two busy women.

Jumping in surprise, Ginny backed into Scott's arms. Her shoulders received a quick squeeze before he released her and turned her around. His smile searched her face. "I see you survived our trip to The Creamery just fine."

"I did, though I can't say the same about Jezebel. We had a pretty late night before her system finally settled down. Eating almost two doggie cones proved to be more than she could handle."

They shared a mutual smile as he clasped her hand in sympathy for her ailing dog. "Are you part of the businessmen's club, Scott?"

"Just for today--after we parted last night, Edmund called and said you would be here for the presentation. It didn't take his usual amount of persuasion to convince me I should come and support you."

Remembering that Scott had come into the musical production through Edmund's coercion gave Ginny a moment of doubt. She hoped he had come today as a willing participant. Gazing his way, her doubts faded when he smiled his full support. Edmund called out her name and the presentation began.

❤ ❤ ❤

"So, you can see that your money will be well spent if you choose to become our sponsors for items like the costumes on display here. Not only will we use the clothing in the musical, but afterwards the Forest Glen Historical Museum will put the outfits to good use. Their volunteers will be able to wear the costumes for special holiday events and for their presentations to the school children who come to the museum for field trips."

Edmund suggested a donation amount and the group overwhelmingly voted to give the gift to the musical in exchange for advertisement in the program. Several business owners brought up the idea of buying individual advertising space for their own companies and donations began flying in from around the room.

The well-prepared Edmund had forms for everyone, and his secretary set up a station in one corner of the room to collect their checks. Several of the businessmen and women even asked about auditions, saying they had always dreamed of acting in a play after enjoying their roles in high school dramas or musicals in the past.

Scott excused himself to head off to his campers. Ginny appreciated his support but still struggled with completely trusting any man. After all, Edmund had coerced Scott to direct the musical. Did the benefactor force him to attend this morning's breakfast? Scott had indicated not, but he seemed relieved to head off to camp. New supporters gathered around the two women and she focused on greeting them. Their backing would provide a definite boost toward funding the program. Now, if only that could continue...

❤ ❤ ❤

At the next meeting of the production committee, everyone

seemed to have good news. Ginny grew more excited with each report.

"I can hardly believe the generous donation from the hospital auxiliary." Grace Cole waltzed into the room and laid their check on the table for everyone to admire. "Besides their monetary gift, the hospital recently had several murals painted within the building and there is an abundance of leftover paint. They are willing to donate those supplies to the set committee."

"That is great. Hopefully the paint is colors we can use." Scott picked up the hospital check and passed it to David as he expressed his thanks to Grace. "My church approved use of their copier for printing the scripts. Honey rounded up a crew of her pals to supervise the printer and put scripts into folders."

Annie modeled a frilly petticoat over her business clothes as Ginny reported, "Miss Hope and the Needlers from First Church have completed enough one-size-fits-all petticoats to hold out the historical skirts for up to twenty women." Bright bows and ribbons adorned the undergarment, marking the influence of Ginny's creative mother.

Kim Ericson shared a scrapbook of her *Kim's Komments* articles and other writings that appeared in the paper. As everyone oohed and aahed over her work, Ginny asked, "Would you be willing to become the official photographer and historian for the event? Your scrapbook is a great start."

"It would be my pleasure. I'll be sure to keep you in the news as much as I can, too," Kim responded.

Edmund Bradley proudly presented his own enormous gift of support along with the funds collected at the business meeting. Mayor Kyle and David Ericson, the county representative, brought the promised checks from their respective government branches. Ginny leaned over David's shoulder while he tallied up the donations, as the committee's acting treasurer. Each check meant success for both the musical and the museum. She laced her hands together in a silent prayer.

When David announced the total, she lifted her hands in praise to God and turned to hug Annie and then Scott. They had enough support to begin purchasing materials for building sets and making costumes--once the actors auditioned. Surrounded by the cheering committee, Ginny realized she still clung to the professor's arms. A tingle spread through her chest as she backed away from Scott, who reached for her hand and held on when Edmund called the meeting to order.

As everyone returned to their spots around the museum's mahogany table, David presented several poster designs for advertising and the committee voted on their favorite, giving the go-ahead for production to begin on the printing. They formed several sub-committees to work under Ginny and Scott's direction. They also gave the okay for everyone to begin advertising, creating, and doing everything necessary to make the musical a success. Ginny and Scott shared a happy smile and their joined hands added a warm sensation under her already exalted emotions.

Scott stayed after the meeting to help the ladies clean up the museum. "Is there anything else you need help with, ladies?"

Annie raised her eyebrows as she turned toward Ginny. "Someone needs to lay claim to this guy. Anyone willing to help clean up this mess is a keeper, in my book."

"It sounds like I'll be keeping our pizza date this weekend." Ginny winked at Scott as he wrapped an arm around her waist and then they danced around the room.

♥ ♥ ♥

"Hey, can you pass me another piece of pepperoni?" Don Drummond held his plate up for the requested slice as he put his arm around his pregnant wife and gave her a loving squeeze. "I'm eating for two, you know."

"That's right. He's eating my part of the pizza since I can't seem to stand any spicy food lately." Ellen only half laughed as she sipped her lemon water and played with a handful of crackers. She grinned and added, "I think he's going to gain more weight than me."

As everyone laughed at Don showing off his growing belly, Ginny studied the happy couple and wondered what it would be like to have a child of her own. Would she have a little girl with long, wavy curls, or a little blue-eyed boy with reddish blonde hair? When she bumped shoulders with Scott, sitting cozily next to her in the crowded booth, she blushed at the direction her thoughts had taken. After all, she'd only known him for a short time and couldn't believe she already had thoughts dancing through her head about children. Her kids at school and Jezebel should be enough "little ones" for now. Distracting herself by selecting another slice of pizza, Ginny reined in her thoughts and concentrated on getting to know Scott's Bible study group.

Watching him interact with his friends over the meal had been a nice revelation. He volunteered to lead the group in blessing their food that evening. The words of thanks demonstrated a close relationship between the man and his heavenly Father and Savior Jesus. When plates and hot pizza arrived, Scott had proved himself a true gentleman as he made sure everyone else got what they wanted before he made his move to fill his own plate. As the end of the evening drew closer, he stacked plates in the center of the table in a gesture toward assisting the waitress with her cleanup.

"Who taught you to be so perfect? You're making the rest of us men look bad tonight," Don laughingly teased as Scott brushed crumbs into a plate.

"Like I told Ginny, my mom raised me well. I also had several waiter jobs while I worked my way through school. You'd be amazed at how many aspiring drama majors end up serving tables."

"I imagine it took a lot of acting skills to deal with some customers." Ellen looked pointedly at her loving husband, who had amassed a messy pile of pizza crusts on a crumpled napkin.

Don deftly changed the subject by asking Scott about his involvement in the world of drama. Everyone laughed at some of the more humorous things he experienced as both an actor and a director. When the evening drew to a close, Scott and Ginny rode home in the middle seats of Don and Ellen's new mini-van.

"I hope you are enjoying our new mode of transportation. We traded in our little red sports car for this beauty." Don laughingly joked about the old red clunker that had been with him since college days.

"Somehow, I don't think an old Cavalier qualifies as a sports car," Ellen teased her husband.

"Well, I drove it to all the sports events during our college years," he quipped back.

Scott gave Ginny's hands a squeeze when they walked to her door. Don's tooting horn from the driveway separated the two, who smiled and parted ways with a quick hug. When Scott returned to the mini-van, Ginny gave a final wave from her porch and laughed as Don revved the engine of his "sporty" new van and drove off into the evening.

Chapter 11

The next morning as she took Jezebel for an early Sunday morning trot around the neighborhood, Ginny found herself praising God with all her heart for the way everything had fallen together. Sniffing the air, Jezebel let out a friendly howl as they passed Scott's house.

"Sorry hound dog, it looks like they aren't early risers like us. We'll see Scott in a couple of hours when he comes to pick me up for church."

Ginny dragged the reluctant dog down the street, around the block, and back to her home. Taking a quick shower, she chose a favorite pair of pants and topped it with a lacy feminine blouse. Looking through her jewelry collection, she chose a necklace made of colorful polished stones her mother had created as a birthday gift and looped it around her neck. As she dressed, Ginny warmed up her voice by singing through the song she and Hope would be sharing later that day.

Woooof, Jezebel howled out a greeting when Scott pulled up in the driveway and then made his way onto the porch. Ginny opened the door before he could knock and laughed about her built-in doorbell, or should they say door howl? Jezebel rolled over on her back as she offered her belly for a scratch from Scott. After a ritual belly rub, Ginny secured Jezebel in her laundry room lair. Then they made their way to Ginny's church.

The little brick church was very different from the large one Scott attended. They had no band, but the pianist who sat absorbed in her music played the instrument enthusiastically and with a lot of soul. Everyone knew each other personally and when Ginny walked in with Scott at her side, they found themselves surrounded and greeted.

"This is Scott Hallmark. He's going to be the director for *Incident at Woodson House.*" Ginny made a general introduction as members of the congregation introduced themselves.

"You better do right by our Ginny, we know she worked real

hard on that musical and you gotta make it the best you can 'cause we're really proud of our girl." Miss Hope's elderly mother poked her cane in Scott's direction, giving him her mandate. "And if you get any other ideas about our girl, you better be good to her or I'll personally come after you with my walking stick."

Ginny rocked from one foot to the other as Scott gently took the older woman's hand.

"I promise to be good to her, ma'am, so you can hold on to that stick. By the way, I'm looking forward to hearing your lovely daughter sing with Ginny today. I've discovered that your Hope is quite a talented lady, too."

The elderly woman grinned at the mention of her daughter and invited Scott and Ginny to join her in a favorite pew. Always the gentleman, Scott allowed the ladies to enter the auditorium and pew ahead of him.

The small congregation belted out their songs of worship with full voices that reverberated around the little sanctuary. When Hope and Ginny sang their song as an offering to God, voices from the congregation rang out with hearty "Amens" of thanks and appreciation for the message they presented. Then the minister brought a message about different ways God provides love in the lives of His children. Ginny and Scott became the recipients of many glances when the preacher brought up the subject of love between a man and woman.

Exiting the church proved to be a long, drawn out event as everyone got to know Scott better and expressed their thanks to Hope and Ginny for their special music.

"Such a sweet song! I love it when you two sing."

"Always glad to have someone new visit. It looks like we had several visitors today."

"We hope you'll come back soon."

Surprise filled Ginny's heart when the Russell family approached and a bold Melissa gave Scott an enthusiastic hug while babbling about how much fun she had at theater camp. "Can we do the trip to the moon activity again? I loved it."

Many of the church members ended up eating at a home-style diner located within walking distance of the church. Scott and Ginny sat at a table near Hope and her mother, sharing conversation with people seated around them at other tables. A tall, lanky man scooted in next to Hope.

"I don't believe we've met before." Ginny shifted her eyes between the man and Hope.

"This is Bill. He manages the displays at the City Art Museum. He's been looking for a new place to worship." Hope stammered slightly as she introduced her friend.

When they left the restaurant, Scott commented on the friendly bunch. "I really enjoyed meeting everyone from your church. It was like going to a big family reunion."

"That's one of the best things about my church. I feel needed and wanted when I go there to worship. Their love and caring spirit encourage me every Sunday."

They continued their conversation as they traveled home. When Scott stood at Ginny's door, he gave her a quick peck on her cheek.

"Don't forget to come early for the auditions next week. I probably won't see you until then, since I promised my parents I'd spend the Fourth of July at their place."

Ginny stood on her porch as he drove away. Dreamily touching the cheek Scott had kissed, she smiled to herself and then twirled around in celebration. When she opened her front door, it became evident that Jezebel had escaped the laundry room. The dirt-covered dog stood happily digging in the houseplant that formerly sat near the front door. Ginny wanted to be angry at the animal, but instead she bubbled with laughter as she looked for the broom and dustpan.

❤ ❤ ❤

Celebrating the Fourth of July had always been a tradition for the Cline family. Ginny and Jezebel made their way to her mother's home and arrived with a cooler full of potato and fruit salads. She followed the scent of grilling burgers as she wheeled her loaded ice chest behind her small childhood home. Her mother's friend, Roy, waved to her from his spot at the gas grill. Her brother stood nearby, unloading buns and condiments from grocery bags. He added his donation to Mom's desserts already on the picnic table.

The aroma of baked beans wafted through the sliding screen door where her mother stood in the kitchen, stirring a pitcher of fresh lemonade. Giving Roy a hug, Ginny couldn't help but comment on the frilly apron he wore over his Cincinnati Reds tee-shirt and jeans.

"Looks like you're losing your touch when it comes to aprons. Mom's going to have you wearing ruffles in public before you know it."

"I had my Heavy Duty Griller apron on until about an hour ago, and then Snoops had a little accident. I tried to help your mother put the baked beans in the oven when her dog and I had a difference of opinion. I lost, the beans went all over the place, and Snoops got a heaping serving of beans in his face--not that he minded. So my usual apron is in the laundry and Snoops is in the dog house, literally."

Roy laughed at his play on words. His kind Christian spirit had filled a hole in their lives during the last few years. Her deadbeat birthfather left a great chasm when he abandoned their family and headed for a lifetime of pleasure. His choices led to a lifestyle that eventually killed him. Roy placed an hand on her shoulder and held her at arm's length as he searched her face.

"There's something different about you today, Ginny. Is there anything that you would like to tell this old man?"

"You're not that old, Roy."

"And you're avoiding my question." Roy meant well, but Ginny hesitated. She trusted him more than most men, but...

"So what is new, sis?" Her brother, Nathan, added his voice to the questioning as Ginny's mom also stepped into the fray.

Giving Jessie a welcoming hug, Ginny smiled as she began to share the successful progress of the musical. "Thanks to Mom, we have some beautiful petticoats for the ladies." When she mentioned Professor Scott Hallmark, her demeanor must have changed because the whole family began to question her in earnest as she described his involvement and admitted to her growing interest in the gentleman.

"Is the man in question a Christian?" Roy crossed his arms, playing the protective parent role well.

"Yes, he is, and he seems very involved in the church that he attends. Which by the way is a sister congregation to ours. He came to church with me last week, when you and Mom were gone to a book signing."

"Then you should have invited him to come to our Fourth of July get together today." Mom couldn't hide her smile. "That way we could get to know him better."

"We've only known each other for a few weeks. Half of that time, I didn't even like him." Ginny tried to convey disinterest, but she couldn't stop the warmth that spread across her cheeks.

"Watch out, sis, they'll have you marching down the aisle if you aren't careful. So where is your honey this weekend?" Nathan couldn't resist putting in his two cents as he gave her a teasing smirk.

"Honey is probably over at her church practicing away on her electric bass and Scott went to his parent's home for the holiday." Ginny burst into laughter at their confused expressions, then told her family about the lovely little lady named Honey. When she related her feelings of jealousy over the unknown mysterious woman, Mom and Roy shared a look that let Ginny know they were thinking Scott might be her Mr. Right. Growing tired of being the center of attention, she turned the tables on her brother with questions, and discovered he had recently begun dating someone. Teasing Nathan and encouraging Mom to ask him questions provided a welcome relief and gave her time to reflect on her own situation with Scott.

After finishing their picnic, the Cline family packed the leftovers into the refrigerator and left for the city park to view Fourth of July fireworks. As Ginny gazed at the bright patterns of light that lit up the dark sky, she couldn't help but wonder if Scott and his family were enjoying their holiday in the same way.

♥ ♥ ♥

Scott stretched out on the blanket his parents had provided for the occasion. Watching fireworks on the Fourth of July at the local fairgrounds had always been a great way to celebrate. Listening to the small community band play traditional Sousa marches from the gazebo at the center of the fairgrounds made him think of the much smaller gazebo on the grounds of the Forest Glen Historical Museum. Whistling along to a lively rendition of *Stars and Stripes Forever*, he thought of pleasant hours recently spent there.

Ginny had pranced around the structure as she enthusiastically described the importance of the little town in the Underground Railroad. He had absorbed most of what she said, but the sun glinting off her wavy hair had filled his thoughts. Though normally a deep brown, the sun had brightened her tresses in a way that brought out red highlights. His mind strayed to the question of whether their children would have red hair.

Laughing now at where his memory wandered, he mentally scolded his distracted mind. He did not need to focus on what might be, unless she actually agreed to a more permanent relationship. Still it was nice to dream about the pretty lady.

"Hey, are you all right? You're looking kind of goofy for someone who's supposed to be cheering on the fireworks," his brother, Robert, teased.

"Sorry, my mind was on another kind of fireworks. The female kind..."

"Did I hear right? The eternal bachelor is experiencing fireworks over a girl! Hey everybody, Scott's in love!"

Before Scott could stop his tornado of a brother, the whirlwind of news spread throughout the groups of cousins and friends reclining on blankets surrounding the brothers. In only a matter of minutes, the people gathered in nearby lawn chairs joined in the teasing. Everyone momentarily forgot the fireworks in the sky, and began their own show, blasting Scott with one question after another about his girl.

As the show in the air wound down, Scott helped his parents pack blankets and chairs into the trunk of their car. Courtney Hallmark leaned close and drew her eldest son to her side in a warm hug. "I wish you happiness, son. I've been praying all your life that you would find a sweet Christian woman to love you with all her heart. I'll continue to pray that if Ginny's the one, the relationship will come together for you both, in God's time."

"Thanks, Mom. I just hope we can find the kind of happiness that you and Dad experienced in your lifetime."

"Hey, we're not dead yet." Mom gave Scott a loving punch on his arm and joined George in the front seat of their car for a big kiss in front of their two sons.

"Cut it out, Mom and Dad. You'll give us kids ideas," Robert teased in a voice that mimicked something from their childhood.

Taking a cue from his mischievous brother, Scott joined in the banter. Soon the foursome laughed heartily as the old sedan puttered its way back to the family homestead. As they pulled into the drive, Carlos' welcoming yaps filtered through the window of Scott's old bedroom. Adding to the din were the howls of Roscoe, the family dog. Using Roscoe and Carlos' need for a walk to escape his family's friendly harassment, Scott strolled around the old neighborhood, wishing he had asked Ginny to come with him for the weekend to meet his family. Breaking the news to them only reinforced his desire to grow closer to the entrancing author of *Incident at Woodson House.* He would have plenty of opportunity once auditions started.

Chapter 12

Ginny stood alone on the stage. She blew out a huff of nervous breath before she began reading the monologue for female auditions. Giving an emotional appeal to an unseen listener, Ginny threw herself into the lines she had written. She held a hand to her heart as she begged for assistance aiding travelers in their escape from a life of slavery.

"Bravo," Scott cheered as she finished. "I would ask if you could sing something for me, but I've had the pleasure many times in the last few weeks. So, why don't you come on down and we'll review how we're going to handle the rest of the auditions."

Sitting at the small table set up in front of the stage, Ginny and Scott put their heads close together. They reviewed the forms to use for recording abilities to act, sing, and follow simple movement associated with the play. Scott's hand brushed Ginny's as he handed her several pencils. They both paused to share a caring look before sounds of a growing crowd in the building's foyer drew their attention.

Annie sat outside the door of the auditorium, serving as the greeter and official paper pusher for the audition forms. Being Annie, she had the waiting people organized into groups and time slots. She would bring the potential actors in promptly at their appointed time, and then have them sit in the back of the auditorium while they waited for Scott and Ginny to finish evaluating the previous auditions. After that, a small auditioning group would do a movement activity together. Soon the parade of talented people began to make their way to the stage, giving it their best as they acted and sang.

♥ ♥ ♥

Ginny clapped her hands with pleasure when several of her students from the past year auditioned. Her heart went out to sweet Melissa, who had blossomed in the Russell family's loving home. When the child stepped onto the stage, she did so with a new air of confidence and health as Mr. and Mrs. Russell cheered her on from their seats in the auditorium. Melissa's bronzed cheeks, which reflected her African and European ancestry, boasted a sun-kissed look as the happy child sang and read a few lines from the script.

When Miss Hope and Melissa portrayed the runaway and her child, Scott looked at Ginny and they both nodded, acknowledging they had found the right twosome to play the roles.

"Melissa's confidence has changed so much since the first day of camp. I'm glad the campers and I could be part of her growth," Scott whispered to Ginny as the young girl stepped boldly from the stage. He reached out to give the child a fist bump when she passed their table.

Hope stood alone on the stage, ready to audition for the singing part of her role. "I'd like Ginny to join me on stage. I want to use the duet we sang at church for my audition, if that's okay."

"I'll join you if you agree to do the verses alone." Ginny wanted Scott to evaluate her friend's excellent voice on its own.

Hope nodded her agreement and Scott waved Ginny to the stage. As they sang, both women seemed to forget the world around them. As the two friends put their all into the music, they drew the audience in with them. When the melody ended, the group sitting at the back of the auditorium burst into loud applause. Giving each other a quick hug, Hope went out the side door to hurry back to her shop and Ginny took her place next to Scott as auditions continued.

Ginny forced her hands to stop shaking and then looked for the next name. "Here comes another one of your protégés." She laughed as Derrick's energetic spirit filled the stage. His quick humor and even his tendency to push the rules to their limits demonstrated that the boy would be a leader someday, if he wasn't already! His leadership skills had grown apparent in her classroom. Thank goodness, he'd decided flannel shirts and jeans were the in thing for guys during the weeks preceding last year's first Ohio history field trip. There had never been so many boys willing to dress in flannel before.

Ginny highlighted his name on her papers. Derrick's talents would fit well in one of the longer children's roles she had added into the revised script. He had the memory of an elephant and the courage of a lion, so taking on any role would be easy for him. Before going to sit with the group in the back of the room, he bounded over to Ginny and gave her the complicated handshake he had used in her class.

Susanne twisted and turned as she danced across the stage. Her slightly off-tune voice rang out sweetly as she sang *Jesus Loves Me* to her own tempo. She would make an enthusiastic chorus member, as long as she didn't sing too loud.

The mayor's nephew turned out to be quite an entertainer as he sang a rousing rendition of *If I Only Had A Brain*, complete with a comedic scarecrow dance across the stage. Mayor Kyle, who had transported his nephew to the audition, dramatically read a few lines, saying he would be glad to do a small non-singing role, if they needed him.

School secretary Denise and fellow teacher Kara laughed their way through a duet and expressed their support for Ginny's not-so-secret project. Several middle-aged women and three older gentlemen from the business club auditioned for speaking roles. Based on their Barber Shop Quartet background, the men informed Scott and Ginny they were not interested in singing solo, but they would gladly sing harmony in choral situations. Several members of Scott and Ginny's churches also came out to audition for adult roles, including Hope's friend Bill, who fit the role of the husband in the runaway family.

After individuals finished auditioning, Scott taught each small group a simple dance step for the musical. Susanne excelled and acted as a teacher to Derrick and Melissa. They learned quicker than the adults. Scott had the children stand in the front row so the others could follow their lead.

As the time for auditions neared its end, it became clear that Ginny might not have a choice when it came to taking the leading lady's role. Thoughts of stage fright waged war with possibilities as Ginny looked upward toward the Lord for strength.

Then Melody walked in the door. The music teacher from Forest Glen Elementary winked at Ginny. "I am glad your musical isn't a secret anymore. I'm so excited to have a chance to be part of your production. You should be proud of what you're doing for the community."

Her rendition of *You'll Never Walk Alone* filled Ginny with awe, and a confusing rush of relief-filled disappointment. Melody's final note rang throughout the auditorium as Scott applauded. It looked like the leading female role would belong to the talented music teacher. Ginny didn't have to worry about performing the major part, so why did she have such a sinking sensation in her midsection? She blamed it on the lack of any qualified leading men, other than Scott.

She pushed that thought aside. Knowing the hours for auditions were almost over, she stacked her copies of application papers and placed them in a folder. She voiced her concerns as she turned to Scott. "Guess you might be the leading man after all."

"No worries. I saw an old acquaintance last night when Edmund and I met for an update at Carl's Coffee House. James just moved to the area and has been in numerous productions. He might be the perfect leading man for this musical."

James. A sliver of fear pierced her heart. *Surely not...*

"He had a commitment tonight and said he might be late. If he doesn't make it, perhaps we can meet with him on another day."

The custodian entered the room and began to pick up forgotten sheet music. He turned some of the house lights down and shadows filled the space.

"Guess we better take our cue and call it a day," Ginny said. Then the auditorium door burst open and a man's voice rang through the room. A voice she knew all too well.

"Sorry I'm late, Scott. Do you still have time for me?" The dark-haired, well-built guy looked picture perfect for a leading man's role. The low lighting emphasized his high cheekbones. Despite that, Ginny refused to give him a chance. Not after what he'd done in the past.

"I didn't have time to fill out your audition sheet, but here's my acting resume if you'll accept it."

The man laid down the sheet of paper in front of Scott. Ginny could see it enumerated a long list of plays and musicals he had participated in over several years.

Scott didn't seem to notice her angst as he reached out a welcoming hand. "I'm glad you could make it, James. Tell me about this new career you mentioned last night."

"My 'act' now includes the role of pharmaceutical sales representative. I suppose you could say I'm a professional actor with a healing hand. My new territory includes Forest Glen. I'm glad I ran into you last night, because I'm looking forward to acting again. Is this the amazing creator you mentioned?"

His expression fell when he stepped back from the table, his shadow no longer hiding Ginny's face.

"Ginny!" His Adam's apple bounced nervously in his neck. "I didn't realize... Look, I'm sorry for everything." His face expressed sadness, but she could not believe he felt any sorrow. "I didn't realize... Maybe I should go --"

Ginny stopped his speech with hands in the air. She glared at the two men."I can't believe you two know each other." Her hands clenched as she placed them in her lap and fought for control. Her betrayer stood waiting to audition.

Her worst nightmare had come true. He looked like a leading man, but the liar's presence could only mean trouble, with a capital T. James had deceived her before. She refused to let him do it again. Her pen stabbed into the resume, as she scribbled, **No**. *Not a choice, even if we have to use Grandpa Warren to be our leading man.*

"Excuse me, Ginny, may we speak in private?" James' hand trembled as he beckoned her to step from behind the table.

Raised eyebrows gave evidence of Scott's curiosity and concern as he rose and crossed his arms. "Whatever needs to be said can be told to both of us."

"I need to apologize for the past. I did Ginny a terrible injustice back in college. I need to beg for forgiveness." James sounded sincere, but he had always been a great actor.

"I'm not sure I can trust you. I thought you would do the right thing back in school, and you betrayed me by using what I created to save your grade from disaster. You left me in the shadows while you took the spotlight and ran away with the show." Ginny spat the words out and slapped her hands on the table.

"First, I need to congratulate you on your new show. I'm sure it is a quality piece, even without reading the script. The one I stole from you took me farther than I could have dreamed. If it's any consolation, my actions have been burning a hole in my conscience since then. The shame has been eating at my soul for years. I'm finally on a new path with a renewed faith." James hesitated before continuing. He seemed to be calculating his next words. " Please give me a chance to make some amends. If I can help by acting in this musical, I'll give you my best. Maybe it can atone for the past. I'm sorry. I know I can't say that enough. And I promise to help instead of destroy this time around."

"I don't know..." Ginny knew she should forgive, but couldn't force herself to shape the words.

"I'm not the selfish man you knew in college. Please believe me when I tell you I'm sorry. This is your chance to shine. I won't betray you again. You have a witness this time." James turned hopeful eyes toward Scott.

Scott replied, "Give us a minute."

"Sure." James stepped to the back of the auditorium as Scott laid his arm across Ginny's shoulders.

"What was all that about?" Scott asked.

"We worked on a project together when we were in college. I did all the work and he got all the credit, until things started going wrong under his direction. He convinced everyone that I was causing the problems. I was too shy back then to stand up for myself. Once things started working in his favor, he took the honors. James left me sitting in the dust when he took my musical skit to a contest, as his own. I ended up doing make-up assignments to save my grade for that semester. I lost the friendship of several people, including that of my betrayer, James." A tear trickled down her check and then she stared at Scott. "I can't believe you invited him to audition."

"Sorry, I didn't know. If my opinion matters, his apology seems sincere. He did his best when I worked with him a few years ago. Besides, we may have to give him a chance. I haven't seen any other leading men walk through the door tonight." Scott removed his arm and a chill wrapped around her shoulders as he stood. He paced in front of the table and tugged at his chin.

She hugged her arms to her chest. "I just don't know if I can trust---or forgive him." There, she had stated the true problem: forgiveness. Ginny knew she needed to heal, and forgiveness provided a way out of her hurt. God expected her to forgive, but she struggled to make the right decision.

"Do you want me to ask James to leave?" Scott met her gaze with compassion.

"No. We can at least listen to his audition. We do need a leading man for Melody. Just promise me you will study the part, in case he acts the traitor and dumps us at the last minute." Ginny hated to admit that James might be an answer to her prayers for a complete cast. She just hoped he was sincere and still had enough talent to play the role. Heaven help them all if he planned to ruin her musical again. Her days of being timid were quickly fading.

"I'll be his understudy if you agree to be Melody's. That way you can have the assurance of success this time."

Ginny nodded her agreement as she fought her doubts about the man. Scott seemed to think James would do his best. Maybe forgiving him would open up her soul to trust again. She knew what the Lord expected, even if it terrified her.

♥♥♥

Scott watched Ginny walk back to James. He couldn't understand their quiet conversation but overheard the words "conditional" and "forgive" as James reached out and took her hand in both of his. Scott cleared his throat, fighting not to interfere. She broke contact, her finger wagged at the man like he was a student and she his teacher. Good girl. Her stiff posture said more than words as they headed back toward the stage. Scott forced himself to focus on James' resume. The man had racked up some impressive credentials, ones that would improve the musical if he followed through. He'd been ideal in the play they did together.

Ginny's eyes seemed to follow James as he stepped onto the stage. A not so accidental bump from Scott's knee brought her focus back to the resume that he shoved in her direction. One minute the woman seemed ready to throw the man out with the trash. The next, she seemed lost in her thoughts as she stared at the guy. Had he made a mistake by taking a chance on this experienced actor?

"Impressive resume, but we'll want to see what you can do before we decide if we need more information. You'll still have to sign our release and fill out the other audition materials." Scott's voice sounded strained to his own ears. Ginny raised her eyebrows, as she looked his way and then turned her gaze to the actor with an unreadable expression. Focusing on James, Scott gruffly indicated they were ready to hear him sing.

Giving the pianist a smiling nod to begin, the man crooned his way through a song that ran through both tenor and bass ranges. As he read a portion of the script, his voice resonated throughout the room and even the custodian paused to listen. Scott admitted to himself that the man still had talent. He would be a great addition to the musical. However, Scott did not like the idea of putting the fellow in the same room with Ginny, based on their history and her worried expression.

"Thank you, Mr. uh...Early." Scott did a double take as he read James' surname on the resume. He had not remembered the man's last name from when they worked together before. He found himself laughing at the fact that Mr. Early came late to the auditions. Then he stifled his mirth as he remembered his mixed feelings about the man who currently seemed to be studying Ginny.

Scott abruptly closed the notebook that contained comments and stood up to dismiss the man. "You'll need to check the website that we've established for the musical's audition announcements, Mr. Early."

"Please call me James. We worked together before, and Mr. Early seems a little formal for the theater setting, don't you think?" James' glance passed from Scott and came to a rest when he faced Ginny's direction. "I won't let you down, Ginny. I promise."

"I hope so," Ginny replied with a tentative smile that set Scott on edge.

"Thank you for giving me a chance. I really hope I can be of service to you as an actor in the musical." He extended his hand, which Ginny stiffly shook, and then he turned to Scott, who reluctantly accepted the courtesy.

After releasing James' hand, Scott possessively clasped Ginny's fingers. He didn't fight a triumphant grin when the man glanced at their intertwined fingers and his expression fell slightly.

"Thanks for coming. I'm sure you'll be hearing from us soon." Ginny released Scott's hand as the man walked from the room. He grimaced as she turned to look at his scowling face. "What was that all about? You could have told him tonight we need him for the lead role--unless you doubt he is sincere? You're the one that invited him and assured me he would do a good job." Worry lines flickered across her face as she searched his eyes.

"That's not the way it's done in theater," Scott groused. "Besides, he made us stay late because he couldn't show us the courtesy of coming in on time."

"You told me he had his reasons for being late. Anyway, it doesn't seem as if there's much choice here unless you want Grandpa Warren or Derrick to take the lead role. There is that tall skinny guy from your church, but I think we better keep him on speaking roles unless we want to break windows. Of course, there are those three high school boys. Maybe one of them will do, unless... Would you consider doing the role yourself?" Ginny's questioning expression seemed to beg his agreement as she waited for an answer.

"Ginny, I'm sorry. If Edmund hadn't hired me to direct, I'd be honored to play your leading man, in more ways than one, by the way. As it is, James is ideal for the role. I guess I did overreact." Reaching out for Ginny's hands, Scott prayed she would understand what he meant.

She accepted his open palms and smiled. "Trust me when I say that man ruined my life once. It won't happen again. I'll be watching him like a symphony conductor. If he plays so much as one wrong note, he'll be packing his music and leaving. You weren't getting jealous of James, were you?"

Scott wiggled his eyebrows as relief filled his chest. "When I saw you staring at him with your mouth hanging open like a wide mouth bass, I couldn't help but get a little jealous." Puckering up his lips, and opening and closing them several times, Scott made a dramatic impression of the gaping mouth of a fish.

Pretending to pout, Ginny answered, "I was just amazed that he would show up after our past history. I did not look that goofy."

"I'm not sure. Let me get a closer look." As Scott drew near to inspect her lips, Ginny's eyes drifted closed.

"Excuse me... Did you need me for anything else tonight?" The quiet little woman, hired to play the piano for the auditions, interrupted their connection.

"No thanks," they answered in unison, and laughed. She picked up her satchel and headed for the door, smiling as she went on her way.

"We'll have to continue this conversation when she's safely out the door," Scott whispered. Ginny smiled in agreement.

"I hate to break you folks up again, but I gotta get this building locked down in the next few minutes, so you better scoot." The custodian chuckled and pointed them toward the exit.

The auditorium door swung open and Annie leaned in. "I've got everything out front closed down." She tossed several stray papers from the foyer into the custodian's rolling trashcan and waved. "Good-night, everybody."

"I guess we'll have to take this up some other day. Can we get together tomorrow, to go over the list and make some final decisions about who will play what role?" Scott's chest filled with hopeful longing as he accepted that they needed to call it a night.

"Anytime works for me. The only other commitment I have is giving Jezebel a little attention."

"We wouldn't want to neglect her any, would we?" Scott laughed at the reference to the goofy dog. "I'll give you a call sometime tomorrow, probably after I take care of Carlos' needs in the morning."

Taking the hint from the custodian when he began turning the lights off, they collected their bags and headed for the nearest exit. Scott grabbed Ginny's hand and drew her close, as they stepped into the waiting darkness. "Would you mind if…"

Ginny's upturned face answered his question as he leaned over and gave her a gentle kiss.

"Good night, sweet Ginny. I can hardly wait until tomorrow."

❤ ❤ ❤

"Good night, Scott." Ginny's breathy voice cracked as she tried to make sense of what had just happened. It hadn't been that long since she'd been angry with the man, and now she craved his kisses. Taking a steadying breath, she pulled herself together long enough to find her keys and get into her little sedan. Waving at Scott to let him know she was ready to leave the parking lot, she led the two-car procession back to their neighborhood. Scott slowed to make sure she made it safely into her drive and gave a quick toot on the horn as he headed around the block to his own home.

❤ ❤ ❤

In the weeks that followed, Scott watched James like a hawk, but the man turned out to be the perfect person for playing the lead character, Joseph. He lived up to his apology to Ginny. His acting experience in other plays gave him all the tools he needed to create a memorable and enduring character. When Scott worked with some cast members, James willingly coached Melody and another group of actors in ways to project their voices and create more excitement in the delivery of their lines. James' experience as a sales representative for pharmaceutical supplies also gave him a personal confidence that rubbed off on every cast member who came in close contact with the lead man. Pairing James with Melody in the main roles worked well. Their mutual admiration grew as they worked through the rehearsals.

"Please don't get involved with them, Christine. It could be a matter of life or death for you," James begged as he dramatized his character Joseph's lines.

"I have to do my part, even if it means breaking the law. I can't just stand by and watch them be returned to captivity," Melody answered as she picked up the basket of prop food.

"But you could be arrested. I don't want that to happen. I care for you deeply." James reached for her hand.

Ring, ring!

The somber mood of the scene shattered to the tune of a clanging cell phone. Melody reached into her pocket and glanced at the phone's display. "Sorry. It's my brother. He never calls." Worry lines creased her forehead as she fumbled to unlock the device.

James paced the floor as he rehearsed the next few lines alone.

Ginny turned to ask Scott about staging the next scene when Melody's voice echoed across the room.

"Jeff? Who? What? Oh no!"

Ginny rushed to Melody's side and draped her arm around the trembling woman's shoulders. Between sobs, Melody choked out, "They're dead. There's been a wreck. My brother and sister-in-law are gone. They're not sure the twins are going to make it. I have to go."

"Do you need help?" Kara joined Ginny as they held Melody in their arms.

"No, it's something I have to do myself." Melody's voice shook as she stood and wrung her hands.

"You're in no condition to drive. Let one of us help," Ginny pleaded with the shaking woman.

"I'll fly to Chicago." Melody's voice grew stronger as she grabbed her purse from a chair and headed toward the door.

Denise joined her and wrapped her arm around her friend. "We came here together. I'll get her home and help arrange transportation."

"I'm so sorry, Ginny. This is going to mess up your musical." Silent tears streaked Melody's cheeks.

"Don't worry. You need to go and be there for the twins. That's all that matters right now." Ginny ushered the distraught woman toward the exit.

Scott called the rest of the cast and crew to circle up for a prayer.

"Dear Lord, please watch over Melody as she travels. Guide the doctors as they seek to save the twins' lives. We pray Your blessings for this family in their time of need."

After the prayer, Scott dismissed everyone for the night and announced, "Be here tomorrow at the usual time. Ginny and I will have a plan by then."

♥ ♥ ♥

Ginny stayed behind to clear the littered rehearsal area. The musical had been coming together nicely. Her heart wept for her friend as she contemplated what they would need to do if Melody wasn't able to continue as Christine.

"Ginny, can you take over Melody's role? You have the part memorized and you've filled in several times when she couldn't make a rehearsal." Scott's words wakened both fear and hope as she turned and nodded her affirmation. She had no other choice.

Later that night, Ginny cuddled with Jezebel, praying for Melody and herself. Could she really take on the role and perform in front of a live audience? Doubts coursed through her as she rubbed her hound's velvety ears. "What am I going to do, Jezebel?"

Ping! Her phone interrupted her with a message from Scott.

I don't know if you're still awake, but I wanted you to know that I always thought you would be the perfect Christine. She has your heart and soul. She overcomes her fears and faces them bravely to save others. If anyone embodies her passion and ability to overcome, it is you. Be brave, my dear friend. I have confidence in you and so does the God who inspired you to create and be who you are!

Ginny closed her eyes and prayed, really prayed. She pleaded for courage to do Christine's part. She begged mercies for Melody and the twins. She opened her heart to the Lord, about her struggle to forgive her dad and James. She thanked her Heavenly Father for the friends and family who supported her in both big and small endeavors.

Calm filled her heart as Jezebel pushed in closer to her side.

She would need to be courageous, but with those she loved supporting her, and God giving her courage, *Incident at Woodson House* would not fail because of her fears.

♥ ♥ ♥

"Thanks for the hints, James. Scott's been trying to get me to be a little more passionate about this particular scene. I guess I didn't realize how much using a prop to make a point can really help emphasize a dramatic moment, though I guess I do use props at school in a similar way. I just hadn't thought to apply it to this situation."

Ginny held a pair of shackles in her hands and re-spoke her lines. Hugging the iron manacles to her chest, she put on her most beseeching voice. Begging James, in the role of Joseph, to look at the shackles, she made Christine's plea for his help.

"Think about the man who wore irons like these. Did he deserve this, Joseph? Is there any reason he has to continue being a slave? It shouldn't matter that he has a different color of skin. Doesn't he deserve to be as free as you and me?" Ginny stepped closer as she dramatically pushed the chained cuffs toward James.

"Oh, sweet Christine, you're breaking my heart with your pleas, but is it right for us to go against the laws of our country? We could be arrested and put in chains ourselves if we break the law."

James laid aside the manacles and took Ginny's hands "Great acting, Ginny, you've almost got Joseph convinced to come over to your side. Now let's go back to the big rehearsal room and see if Scott is ready for us."

On the way back to the main room, Ginny couldn't help but ask a little more about her fellow thespian. "So, James, you really don't seem to be the same person you were back in college. What made you change?"

"My conscience ate at me for years. Desperation drove me to steal your skit in college. I was failing and in danger of losing my scholarship. If I had to do it all over again, I wouldn't do anything to hurt you. Taking credit for your creation proved to be the biggest mistake I ever made."

"It brought discord to my life, too." Ginny's voice shook as she remembered trying to save her own grade for the class, after James claimed her work as his own.

"I'm sorry. I messed up. About four years ago, a friend of mine invited me to church. I hadn't been in years. The minister talked about Jesus forgiving our past. I couldn't live with what I had done and decided to change. I didn't know what happened to you after college. I could only pray God would give me a chance to make up for my bad choices, someday."

"Thank you for sharing. I've been fighting against completely forgiving you. In the last few weeks, you have shown good intentions. I think it's finally time I do the right thing and totally forgive you." Peace filled Ginny as the last grip of mistrust flowed out of her mind. Why had she let her lack of forgiveness rule her heart for so long when the release felt so good?

"Thank you. Your forgiveness means the world to me."

"Good." Ginny put one hand on a hip and shook her finger at James. "I'm planning on you doing your best for this musical, buddy."

James feigned a flirtatious manner and grinned. "Are you interested in renewing our friendship?" He straightened an imaginary bow tie and stood up proudly.

Ginny laughed at his goofy actions and then held both hands in the air. "As much as I like how you've contributed to this musical, friend, it's pretty obvious my choices lay elsewhere."

"Oh yeah, does that lucky professor realize what a great catch he has in you?"

"I think so, but we haven't been dating too long, if you can call catching each other between acts a date. But you're avoiding telling me more about yourself, James. Come on, do a little sharing. Perhaps some information that isn't found on your acting resume…"

James turned solemn before answering Ginny's question. "I guess you could say I use acting as an escape. When I was a teen, my mom married a man who resented my presence. He seemed relieved when I got involved in high school musicals because it got me out of their lives for long periods of time."

"How sad." Ginny patted him on his arm as he stared into space, thinking about the past.

Placing both of his hands over his heart, James smiled and replied, "It's all right. Things worked out for the best since drama is now one of my favorite pastimes."

"Don't you have any social life outside of the theater?"

"Well there is a certain lady who works in our main office I'm kind of interested in. She just hasn't seen me as her knight in shining armor yet." James made a gentlemanly bow and kissed Ginny's hand to demonstrate his imagined knighthood.

"Am I interrupting something?" Scott didn't sound happy. "We're ready for you two on stage."

"No problem, we were just catching up on the past." James headed for the main rehearsal area. "I think Ginny will impress you with her improved acting skills."

"James and I have this down pat now, so be ready to be wowed." Ginny's happy smile should have made Scott elated. His frowning face said otherwise. Slightly puzzled at his reaction, Ginny tried to not let it bother her and readied herself to do her best.

Ginny and James took their places on the taped off "stage" area of the rehearsal space and began the scene they'd rehearsed in the other room. Throwing herself into Christine's role, Ginny became the character who kept trying to convince the love of her life to join forces with the Underground Railroad. As the two actors came to the climactic moment of the scene, Scott suddenly called a halt in the action.

❤ ❤ ❤

Ginny stepped outside the rehearsal building, talking to herself as she paced up and down the sidewalk. "Oooh, he's making me so angry. First I'm not putting enough emotion into the character I'm portraying and then he tells me I'm overdoing the theatrics." After having told her students what to do and how to act, she could now empathize with some of their pouting. Pouring herself into the character with all her heart ended up garnering criticism from the know-it-all professor.

In Christine's role, she had portrayed her love for the leading man as she begged him to join the cause of freedom for those escaping slavery. Reaching out to James as he played the role, she'd stared deep into his eyes, and saw that his look of passion matched hers as they reached a crucial point in the play. Scott chose that moment to have a little tyrant meltdown and started in on both of them about backing off a little. Didn't he get that this was the climax of the whole musical and the changing point in the lives of the leading characters?

Instead of taking his directions in stride, Ginny had nearly lost it in front of everyone at the rehearsal. Luckily, a calm Annie stopped by at that moment and suggested everyone take a break for some of her chocolate chip cookies. Ginny opted for an outside break instead, to think through what had happened. Dripping in sweat from the mid-summer heat, Ginny pulled her hair into a knot on top of her head.

She walked up and down the sidewalk, trying to gain courage and calm before going back into the air-conditioned building to face the music. This was her musical and she refused to take Scott's overreaction without a fight. He might be the expert, but he had missed the boat on this one. Entering the building, she spotted her prey and marched up to the unsuspecting man with fire in her eyes.

"We need to talk, Professor Hallmark. Now..."

Scott turned to face the angry woman with remorse in his eyes. "I agree. Can we find some place a little more private for our discussion?" Several curious faces had turned in their direction at the sound of Ginny's stern teacher tone.

"Better do what she says when she talks to you like that." Derrick's young voice piped up. "I know what it means when Miss Cline comes after you using her teacher voice."

Embarrassed to have drawn attention to their conversation, Ginny quickly agreed to Scott's request. She once again removed herself to the sweltering outdoor heat.

"What is going on, Professor? First, you tell me to put more emotion into the acting and then you don't like it. I thought I had finally gotten into Christine's character."

"I'm sorry, Ginny, I truly am. It's my fault. I over-reacted to the situation."

"I'll say you did! What's wrong with you?"

"You're right. Your acting is good--more than good in fact--it is superb. You had me convinced you were falling for the guy and it seemed so real that I..." Scott paused and looked at Ginny with an expression that begged for mercy. "I forgot for a moment you were only acting and, if you want to know the truth, I was flat out jealous that you might be falling for James."

Ginny's mouth fell open as she stared at Scott in disbelief. She didn't know whether to laugh or cry. Should she laugh in happiness because his jealousy proved his love for her, or should she cry because of his lack of trust in her, when she freely acknowledged her growing interest in him? "Trust me, Professor, I am only doing my best to portray the character I developed for this musical. Beyond that, James has become a forgiven friend but there is nothing personal between us that you need to be concerned about."

"I know that now. Please forgive me?" Scott reached out for Ginny and drew her stiff hands into his. "If I didn't care for you so much, I wouldn't have reacted the way I did. Please trust me..."

"Then you need to trust me and know that when I say I'm interested in you, it means that I'm not falling for James or any other man." Ginny knew her voice still sounded somewhat reserved.

Scott ran his fingers through his hair, leaving it a rumpled mess. "Sorry. I just couldn't help the desire to jump into the scene and push him out of the way. I wanted desperately to hold you in my arms and not let anyone else have their hands near you. Please, Ginny, I beg your forgiveness." Scott's puppy dog eyes finally broke through her reserve. Tears fell as she moved into his embrace, where they both stood giving each other strength and forgiveness for several moments.

"I'm sorry too." Ginny sniffed and turned her face up to meet Scott's as they exchanged a delicate kiss.

"Yoo hoo, I hate to break up this little makeup session, but all of my cookies have been polished off by your hungry cast. Unless you want me to take over being director, somebody needs to get in here and organize all these dramatic types." Annie tried to sound stern, but by the time she finished her announcement she grinned from ear to ear, and winked at the reunited couple. "Did I ever tell you that I've done wedding cakes before?" With that comment, the vivacious museum curator held the door wider as hoots and catcalls joined the woman's laughter.

The couple entered the building with countenances that demanded respect. Everyone took their places, doing their best to put the play in great shape for the upcoming performances. Scott and Ginny both agreed the scene causing their disagreement did not require further rehearsal that day.

As they were leaving for the evening, Scott walked Ginny to her car. "Would I be rushing things if I asked you to come with me on Saturday to meet my parents?"

"I would love to meet the parents who raised you to be such a kind gentleman." Ginny smiled up at Scott before adding, "We'll have to stop by my mom's first, though, since I think it would be better if Jezebel stayed with her for the day."

Chapter 13

Scott helped Ginny lift first one end of the basset and then the other into the backseat of his mini-SUV. Who would have thought that it would be a major operation to move Jezebel from one point to another? But the lumbering dog just couldn't make the jump into his vehicle. Ginny threaded a seat belt through Jezebel's harness and the silly beast let out a basset sigh of relief and laid her head down next to the bouncing Chihuahua, who had already worked himself free of the leash that should have been holding him in place.

"Get your little rat a harness and he will stay in his seat longer."

"He may be a rat but at least he's an athletic rat, which is more than I can say for your beast. I don't think my back is ever going to be the same." Scott groaned as he buckled his seatbelt. He started his navigation system, using the address Ginny had given him, despite protesting that she knew the way.

"Watch what you're saying. My mother loves Jezebel and you're about to meet her."Ginny ran her fingers across her armrest and tapped the rhythm to one of her songs

"Okay... Are you nervous, Ginny?

"Should I be?"

"No, but it's the first time I've ever taken a girl home to meet the parents. Are you sure you don't want to bring Jezebel with us all the way to my parents' house?"

"Are you trying to get out of meeting my mom, Scott?" Ginny reached back to rub the whimpering basset hound's ears as they slowed for a stop sign.

"Actually, I'm just trying to save my back from Jezebel." Scott laughed good-naturedly before turning serious. "I love you, Ginny, and I know I'm going to love the woman who raised such a wonderful person."

"I love you too, Scott. I think I loved both the bearded man and the green towel guy from the day that I met you."

"What? I think you've lost me somewhere."Scott flipped on his turn signal and entered an older neighborhood.

Ginny laughed as she revealed her growing interest in the two early images Scott had presented to her when they ran into each other at school and later at the pool.

"So do you like me better with the beard or without?"

"Let me think about that for a while." Ginny laughed as Scott's navigation device signaled the final turn into her mom's drive.

Getting the basset hound out of the car proved easier, as Jezebel sprang from her seat and headed for the house, where Jessie's special doggie treats awaited. Her happy howls alerted Ginny's mom. Before they were halfway to the door of the small shotgun style home, it opened, revealing an older version of Ginny. The resemblance was startling, especially when topped by a wild mane of purple-streaked hair, with glittering toenails peering out from below the brightly colored dress.

"You must be my Ginny's Scott."

Jessie stepped onto the front porch and gave everyone hugs, including Carlos and Jezebel. Following at a more reasonable pace was a longhaired, graying mutt that gave the other dogs a welcoming sniff. Jessie took Scott by his hands and pulled him into her home. He stared at the colorful walls covered in an assortment of crafts, modern art, and paintings of quaint characters. The woman's bright clothing matched her walls. She cleared a spot on a cluttered couch and beckoned her visitors to have a seat.

"I'm sorry Ginny's brother isn't here today, but apparently Nathan had a 'visit to the parents' of his own to participate in today." Jessie smiled knowingly at her daughter and they both shared a laugh.

"It's hard to believe my brother has grown from being a tormentor of anything female, to a desirable young man," Ginny said.

Jessie served them a light brunch of fluffy omelet and banana nut bread as they got to know each other a little better. Scott's compliment about the food being excellent, compared to his usual fare, went well towards winning her heart. Carlos wormed his way into the doting mother's embrace and soon she had him eating out of her hand, literally. The poor dog was going to be bloated if he had any more omelet.

"So you must be pretty serious about my Ginny." Jessie's comment caught Scott with his mouth full, so he had to grab a quick swig of fresh squeezed orange juice before clearing his throat and making his declaration.

"Ma'am, we haven't made any hard and fast decisions, but I will tell you that I love your daughter very much. So much that I thought it was important that I meet her family and ask your blessings as we explore what the future may bring."

"That sounds like a wise choice, young man. Ginny has mentioned that you are a Christian, so I know you will respect her and take good care of my girl."

"Thank you, I will."

Ginny's mom chose that moment to stop talking, wrapped Scott in another hug, and offered him a second serving of omelet.

After eating, they headed outside. Jezebel howled from behind the screen door as she watched Carlos leap into the car. Mrs. Cline's dog, Snoops, joined the chorus and soon the trio of dogs created a mournful lament.

"Why don't you leave the little guy with me? You can pick him up on your way back tonight." Jessie feigned a puppy dog look of her own.

"I guess it wouldn't matter, if you promise not to feed him too much. I think he's about ready to pop." Scott laughed at the protruding belly of his not-so-little dog as he arranged to leave the pup in her care.

"We're alone at last!" Scott wiggled his eyebrows at Ginny once they were back on the road. "I thought that went well. You have a great mother. Please tell me you know how to cook as well as your mom."

"You just enjoyed the only meal she does well. We ate many omelets after my father deserted us. Thanks to my grandmother, who took me in for the summers, I'm a decent cook when I have the opportunity. It's just gotten too easy to throw something in the microwave when you're cooking for one."

"We'll have to do something about that, then. Once this musical is over, you can practice cooking for two any time you want to invite me over."

"How about the master chef cooking dinner for me some time? Aren't most men able to cook these days?"

"Are you talking about me?" Scott continued the playful banter as they traveled across the countryside. When she answered in the affirmative, he admitted to being skilled when it came to grilling, a talent he had inherited from his dad.

The enjoyable conversation made time pass quickly. When they pulled into his parents' drive, the aroma of grilling meat drew them to the backyard, where the picnic table had been set up for an outdoor meal. Waving a spatula at his son, George Hallmark opened his arms to Ginny and gave her a welcoming bear hug. Turning the cooking utensil and grill over to Scott, his father pulled up a couple of lawn chairs and welcomed her to his patio. Taking a bowl of chips and a couple of bottled waters from the picnic table, he made himself comfortable next to Ginny.

"Scott and I built this deck several years ago when he was able to come home for the summer. My son the nomad has been all over this country, but I'm glad he's finally found a place where he can settle down, and perhaps someone who can really help him put down roots for good one day."

"Dad, would you like to check the steaks?" Scott asked.

"No thanks, I'm checking on your pretty girl right now. If you want to come and sit with her yourself, why don't you close the lid on the grill and join us? I'm about to share some interesting stories about a certain mischievous lad."

Pulling up another chair, Scott prepared to be embarrassed by his past as he held Ginny's hand for comfort. Halfway through his dad's tale of a young Scott's effort to sell tickets to a backyard production featuring the two Hallmark brothers, a howl erupted from the front of the house.

"That must be your mother coming back. Roscoe ran over to the neighbors a little bit ago and she went to get him while I watched the food. That dog can be more trouble than he's worth some days."

"Roscoe, come back here this instant!" Courtney Hallmark's panicked voice echoed from the distance as the *thump-thump* of rushing paws drew closer and closer. A furry mess of mud and leaves rounded the corner, running at full speed toward the group on the patio. Roscoe spotted the guest and open bowl of chips immediately and with all the intentions of a good doggie host, made sure that he drowned Ginny and himself with a thorough covering of mud and chips. Happy to have accomplished his task, he placed his paws in Ginny's lap and began chomping away at the chips that were scattered over them both.

Courtney turned the corner at that instant and stood in horror as she stared at the scene. For once, Scott's dad was totally speechless. Scott sat there, too stunned to do anything but gawk at the muddy mess.

♥ ♥ ♥

Ginny started shaking and before she knew it, laughter bubbled from her mouth. She never thought she would ever meet a dog with worse habits than her beloved Jezebel, but it seemed that Roscoe wanted to tie the record. Scott joined in the hilarity as hoots of mirth erupted from his throat. Realizing the humor of the situation, his parents joined in with chuckles of their own. Roscoe bounced from one laughing person to another, covering them all in mud, chips, and grass clippings.

"You should meet *my* dog some time," Ginny spilled out through gut-wrenching laughter.

"Can't be any worse than the one you just met." Scott's mom giggled as she tried to wipe down Ginny with a napkin she'd grabbed from the table.

"I don't know. Jezebel lives up to her name on a daily basis."

"Jezebel? She must be quite the wicked dog." Scott's dad got in on the conversation and soon they were busy comparing dog stories as they cleaned up the mess and found fresh clothes for everyone to wear. Luckily, the parents weren't too different in size from the younger couple.

As a result of the distraction, the steaks proved to be a little dry, but several minutes simmering in an impromptu gravy made them quite tasty. Fresh corn made up for the loss of the chips. Coleslaw from the Hallmarks' backyard cabbage patch completed the picnic they had all anticipated. Apple pie made from the fruit of trees that grew in the front yard topped off their repast as they waited for Ginny and Scott's clothing to make it through a wash and dry cycle.

♥ ♥ ♥

After the meal, Courtney gave Ginny a quick tour of the house and they ended up in the den, looking through picture albums of the family through the years. Ginny smiled as she looked at the images of a young Scott. Scott's mom asked if Ginny liked children.

"I hope so, I have a whole room full of them at school--and yes, someday I would love to have a few of my own."

The two women nodded in quiet agreement, and then continued laughing and adoring the pictures of the young family at play through the years. When the buzzer on the dryer finally sounded, Ginny realized her visit with the Scott's kindhearted mother had drawn to a close.

♥ ♥ ♥

On the ride home, Ginny and Scott enjoyed recalling the events of the day. When they related Roscoe's story to her mom, laughter returned once more. Roscoe had certainly broken the ice at his parents' house and Carlos had won the affection of Jessie during his visit with Snoops and Jezebel. His rounded belly gave testimony to consuming many treats during the eventful day.

♥ ♥ ♥

By the time they returned to town, Ginny dozed in the cushioned passenger seat of Scott's car. Leaning over, he gently kissed her cheek and murmured, "Wake up, sleeping beauty. Your prince has brought you home."

"Mmmmm. I must be dreaming."

Baawhooo. Baahoo. Yap, Yap.

"Nope--not a dream." Ginny stretched and stumbled from the car. "I had a great time today." She leaned on Scott's arm as he walked her and the drowsy basset hound to their door.

"Take care of yourself. I'll be counting the minutes until church tomorrow." Looking lovingly into her dewy eyes, Scott leaned towards Ginny with a kiss full of promise for the future.

Woof. Chaperone Jezebel nudged her way between them, and the couple parted ways for the evening. Ginny stood looking out her window and blew Scott a kiss as he pulled out of the drive. Life was definitely good.

Chapter 14

Melissa and Hope clutched each other in fear as the sound of the slave catcher's howling hound echoed from off stage. Getting into the act seemed to come natural for the pair. They trembled near a plastic bush and sang a song that expressed their worry and weariness as runaways who had traveled many miles away from a plantation in the South.

As Bill joined his bass voice with their higher tones, the pathos of the song wove its way into the hearts of the listening cast. Joining their hands, the runaway family clung together to sing their final chorus expressing hope and trust in their newfound friends, as they made their way to freedom. Ginny and James came to the edge of the stage on cue and stood hand in hand, awaiting the end of the song. Smiling encouragement at the singing trio, Ginny couldn't help but wonder at the transformation that Melissa had undergone. Bravely the youngster belted out her song without fear or timidity. As the song ended, Ginny and James began their lines.

"Joseph, I'd like you to meet some people who need your help."

"But how? I'm not sure there's anything I can do without breaking the law." James crossed his arms as he played the role of the reluctant hero Joseph.

"Sometimes you have to obey God's law rather than man's when it comes to helping a brother and sister in need. Just think about what they've been through; the beatings that they've endured..." Ginny's character Christine begged for understanding from the man who stood before her, resisting her plea.

"Excuse me, mister, do you have anything that can help my Pa's scars?" Melissa tugged on James' coattails and looked up at him with pleading eyes as she played her part.

Looking at the little family with indecision, James stared in horror as Hope lifted her man's shirt to expose a back full of ragged scars. The cast gasped at the realistic creation presented for the first time during a rehearsal. The mayor's daughter, Rylee, had used her artistic skills to create graphic scars across the man's back. Amazed at the horrific scars, the scene came to a halt as people expressed their understanding of the horrors of slavery from the perspective of the present day.

Moments later, Ginny noticed someone missing from the scene. Turning away from the conversation ensuing on center stage, she spotted Melissa softly crying in a dark corner. The child had drawn herself into a small ball of fear, trying to cry without drawing attention. Moving to the girl's side, Ginny drew Melissa into her arms and comforted her with a caring hug. Allowing Melissa to cry until she began to relax, her trained teacher's mind tried to process what might be going through the child's mind. When Melissa finally calmed enough to take a quaking breath, Ginny saw her opportunity to ask a question.

"Would you like to talk about what is bothering you, Melissa?"

"Oh, Miss Cline, I'm so scared. My momma looked all bloody like that when we lived with her last boyfriend. He hit me too. Does that mean we were slaves? I don't want to be a slave." Tears began to fall again as Ginny hugged Melissa and rubbed her back.

"Don't worry, Melissa. You'll never be a slave. We won't let anyone harm you."

The child sniffed a few more times as Ginny reminded her of the loving care the Russell family had provided since early spring.

Hope joined them and added her warm arms to the circle. She soon had them laughing as she told a funny tale of a recent customer in the fabric store. The woman couldn't make up her mind between two very strange prints, which had joined the sale table due to their lack of popularity. When Scott called places, Melissa jumped into her role and played her part with more feeling than ever.

"Great acting, Melissa!" Scott cheered the child on and then turned to Ginny. "I wonder what inspired her all of a sudden."

"I think she realized how free she is from a past that threatened her health and safety," Ginny answered, as freedom flowed through her own heart.

♥ ♥ ♥

Yappity, yap, yap, yap, Carlos bounced with joy as Scott opened the door that evening.

"Have you been missing me, buddy?" Scott scooped up the

bounding bundle of energy and gave the pup a good rubbing on the head. "Sorry I've been neglecting you, pal, but I've got this great gig helping a beautiful lady put on her big play."

Opening the door for Carlos to take a quick visit outside in his recently repaired fenced yard, Scott grabbed a glass of water and stared at his reflection in the dark kitchen windowpane. Smiling at his blurry image, he couldn't resist asking himself a few questions.

"Good evening, self. How are you holding up? I know it's been hard to watch that other man hanging out with your gal, but you're handling it pretty well, if I do say so myself. Well, most of the time anyway." Scott frowned at himself. Using the excuse of a scratch at the back door, he left his reflections, and let his dog inside. He got out a snack for the Chihuahua, who did a begging dance on hind feet.

Kicking off his shoes and changing into sleepwear, Scott wearily climbed into bed to recover from his long day of teaching followed by an evening of directing the play. *Crunch…crack…*what in the world? Scott rolled back out of bed and pulled the sheets back to discover a Chihuahua sized stash of snack bones and dog chow hidden throughout his covers.

As Carlos protested with growls and yaps, Scott cleaned up the bed with a chuckle. He dumped the pile of edibles into the dog's food dish. Leave it to Carlos to make his day longer. Finally settled comfortably in his bed for the night, Scott smiled as he remembered how well Ginny had fallen into the lead role. It certainly helped that she was the writer, but as each day passed, the personality of her character deepened and changed beyond the words written on paper.

Frowning, Scott couldn't help but be reminded of his occasional twinges of jealousy as James developed Joseph's character to effectively counter Ginny's Christine. Willing himself to rein in his thoughts, Scott relaxed, and after a prayer thanking God for all the new people he worked with, he began dreaming for real. His last thoughts focused on a green-eyed beauty dancing across the stage and into his arms.

Chapter 15

The following day as Scott walked from his late afternoon class to the rehearsal, he took a few moments to enjoy the first fall colors beginning to blaze across the campus. The temperatures were finally on the milder side and breezes rustled the changing leaves. His cell phone rang, interrupting the moment of peace. Checking out the screen, he was surprised to see his mother calling. She knew his schedule pretty well and must be trying to catch him between events.

"Hey, Mom, what's up?" Scott couldn't keep the curiosity out of his voice.

"Hi, Scott, I wondered if you could run home for a little bit on Saturday morning--alone."

"This sounds serious."

"It is, but nothing you should be worried about." Courtney cleared her throat as her voice brightened. "In fact, I think you'll be pleasantly surprised. Just don't mention anything to your dad or brother." There was a slight pause, as his mom appeared to be changing the subject. "Ginny seems like a nice person. You must be pretty serious about her."

"I am. In fact, I think she is the one that I want to marry, once my finances are a little more secure." Scott smiled at his first public proclamation of his intentions. "I'm pretty sure she feels the same way, too. Do you like her, Mom?"

"I do. Ginny impressed me when she visited. She jumped right in when it came to doing things. It seemed like she had been a member of our family forever. I don't think anyone has ever volunteered to clean up a Roscoe disaster before." Hilarious giggles emanated from her end of the phone at the mention of the dog's misdeeds.

"I think Ginny's Jezebel prepared her for any dog disaster. Roscoe's muddy spill probably seemed mild compared to some of the things Ginny told me about her pet." Scott conveyed some of the basset hound's antics as he and his mother laughed together over the phone.

Agreeing to visit home early Saturday morning, Scott signed off with his mother, who left him with no idea what was going on. Between activities at the college and the evening practices for the musical, his tight schedule did not allow much leeway. The urgency in his mom's voice had made him curious enough that he'd promised to make the trip home.

♥ ♥ ♥

After a late Friday night rehearsal, Scott dragged himself and the Chihuahua out of bed for the early Saturday morning trip. Tossing Carlos into his new carrier, Scott started the car and made the drive to his parents' home. When he arrived, he left Carlos in his temporary cage in the foyer by the front door. He searched through the eerily quiet house for anyone who might be around. No noise came from his dad's TV. No sounds came from the kitchen. Come to think of it, Scott hadn't noticed his dad's car in the driveway.

"Hello… Mom… Is anyone home?"

A faint voice replied from the basement, "I'm here, Scott, come on down."

Descending the stairs, Scott didn't immediately locate his mom until he noticed a light coming from the storage room in the back corner of the basement. Hidden behind the open lid of an ancient trunk, Courtney sat amid piles of handmade lace, dusty books, and various knickknacks of a bygone era. An ivory jewelry box sat in her lap. Pulling a velvet pouch from the decorative box, she held it to her chest as tears filled her eyes.

"Mom, are you all right?"

"I'm more than all right. It's just that I have something very precious I want to give to you, and to Ginny if she'll have it. I know your finances are a little tight right now, but I didn't want them to keep you from offering your heart to Ginny. This little pouch contains my grandmother's wedding and engagement rings. Granddad's ring is here, too. She wanted to give them to a grandson, but all of her grandchildren were girls. When you were born, you were her first male descendant. Shortly after your birth, she decided to move into an assisted living apartment and gave me this trunk full of family memories.

"She took off these rings and put them in this jewelry box,

which she then placed in the trunk. She asked me to keep the rings here in safekeeping until you needed them. Granddad was gone and she joked about being a free woman with a new start, but I could tell it was tearing her apart. She looked so sad, but now I know she'd be happy if you want to use them for Ginny. I can see Gran up in heaven, kicking her heels with joy that you have found the love of your life."

Opening up the pouch, she held the family heirloom rings out for Scott's inspection.

"They're perfect, Mom. I hope someday Ginny will accept them, because they're beautiful."

"What do you mean, someday, son?"

"My life is so uncertain until I get full tenure. I want to promise her a secure future."

"No one's future is ever certain, Scott. When your dad and I first married, we lived from penny to penny. There were times we both worked two jobs. We did without what some people might call necessities. But we loved each other, and being together was all that mattered."

"What if I don't get tenure or worse, lose my position? I've heard rumors of potential budget cuts...."

"Do you think she would love you any less if you were back working tables at a restaurant again?"

"I'm pretty sure she would love me regardless of my circumstances." Scott accepted the jewelry from his mother's hands. The solid gold of the rings shone with purity and the emerald cut diamond sparkled as Scott held the engagement ring up to the light to see it better. "I have a feeling she will love these rings, especially when I tell her Great-grandmother's story."

"I hope she knows what a good man she's getting. I'm a little prejudiced because you're my son, but I think anyone who marries you will be getting the perfect gentleman."

"Thanks, Mom, you're the greatest." Scott secured the rings in his pocket and wrapped his arms around his mother. "So where's Dad today?"

"I sent him on an errand so we could have this time to ourselves. I knew I would cry and your dad doesn't like to see my tears. Plus, for whatever reason, Grandma wanted it to be a secret between the three of us. I'm not sure why she chose to do it that way, but I've fulfilled my part of the bargain. You can tell anyone about the rings now. Guess she didn't want the other cousins to try to take them away before you had your chance.

"So how are my cousins doing?" Scott's inquiry about his extended family ended up being an hour-long catchup session for family news.

Carlos and Roscoe sounded an alarm, announcing the return of George Hallmark as the front door opened and the sound of heavy footsteps resounded through the wooden floor above their heads.

"Hello, I'm home." George's steps paused and the dog carrier door rattled open.

The *tip-tap* of Carlos's tiny paws joined the bigger thumps of Roscoe's running feet. Scott's mom closed up the trunk as Scott touched the small bag with the rings in his pocket. They both climbed the steps to enjoy a family brunch.

♥ ♥ ♥

Honey waved wildly from the pit as the townspeople on stage struck a pose and sang the final notes of their song, which celebrated the successful passage of the runaways to their next stop on the Underground Railroad. "We need to hear more sound from the lower parts. Not everyone's voice can go up to that last soprano note without screeching like the wicked witch in the *Wizard of Oz*."

Ginny laughed when Honey softened her criticism with a delightful imitation of an old hag's laugh, which made the whole cast snicker. Ellen provided a quick reminder of parts as she pecked through each line on the piano. They rehearsed the ending scene a few more times to meet Honey's expectations, as tech week rehearsals continued with the band, full costumes, microphones, and makeup.

"These are the funniest looking pants I've ever had to wear." Derrick pranced around the stage, wiggling his body into a variety of odd shapes as he modeled the button up pants with lacing up the back seam. Annie insisted on authentic costumes so they could be reused with her museum volunteers. The extra cloth on the back of the pants, which historically allowed the user to grow through several sizes, provided Derrick with extra padding. The bubbled backside became a source of entertainment for the boy. Ginny shook her head and encouraged her former student to make better choices.

Several of the female cast, including Ginny, added fans to their props list. The fans helped them cool down from layers of petticoats under their historically correct dresses and aprons. The air-conditioned stage at the college provided a welcome relief from the warmth of the unseasonably warm fall. Even with the better temperatures, there were still concerns that arose when one of the ladies nearly did an old-fashioned swoon, after donning full costuming and experiencing the warmth of on-stage lighting. Ginny reminded everyone to keep hydrated for the sake of his or her body and the health of their singing voices.

Most of the characters in the musical had only one costume. Ginny's character, however, had several dresses, since she played the lead role, resulting in some quick changes backstage. At least the old-fashioned undergarments served a useful purpose by providing a modest covering during the costume changes. The green print that impressed Scott had been fashioned into a beautiful dress with puffed mutton leg sleeves, a high waist and a lace collar. Ginny loved the little collar, which had been hand-crocheted by Honey. She wondered how the busy woman found time to make the collar between her church duties and the musical. Regardless, she had been very pleased with the delicate accessory, which set off the green of the dress so nicely.

Scott had decided the green dress would be perfect for the proposal scene. Her other dresses consisted of a gingham work dress with a practical apron and a dark blue dress to serve her at night as she scurried through shadows, assisting passengers on the Underground Railroad. Ginny wore the costumes with a modest sense of pride, knowing that she had done most of the sewing on her own dresses, with some assistance from Hope.

Since Ginny had started back to school the first week of September, she relied on Hope to put some final touches on the outfit. Her extra moments in the last two weeks were divided between the musical rehearsals and preparing for school. Thank the Lord, her previous years of teaching provided well-laid plans for instructing the routine reviews typical of the first few weeks of school.

❤ ❤ ❤

Scott willed himself to get through the last week of rehearsal.

Between a new semester starting and finishing up the final weeks of rehearsal before the mid-September production of *Incident at Woodson House,* it seemed that the only time he ever saw Ginny was on stage and in character. Even their occasional commute together had ended after his late afternoon classes started, leaving him only enough time to walk from the classroom building to the on-campus theater for rehearsals.

A quick run home before the afternoon class provided relief for Carlos but didn't provide any relief for his pining heart, since Ginny still had another hour to teach her school children. A hasty hug or quick kiss after rehearsals seemed to be their only contact as Ginny hurried home to get ready for the next day and Scott stayed behind to close down the stage each evening. Even duties at their churches kept them from worshipping together during the last few Sundays.

Scott pulled the rings from the velvet pouch and ran his fingers over the smooth gold. Hopefully, Ginny would welcome his proposal after the busyness of the play faded. He dropped the rings back in their bag and pushed them into his top drawer. He needed to find the perfect time for a proper proposal, and right now there were no moments available in their busy lives.

Chapter 16

On Monday night of the final week, Scott managed to swing Ginny backstage for an evening hug. Lingering with their arms around each other, Scott leaned down to Ginny's welcoming lips and kissed her in a way that told of his deepening love for her.

"We've got to stop meeting like this and have a real date one of these days," Scott teased before kissing her one more time.

"I agree." Ginny smiled and wrapped her arms around Scott's neck. "I never realized how much time this project would take from my life. I'm so proud and happy that everything is coming together for the musical, but as much as I hate to admit it, I'll be glad when it's over and we can go on a real date for a change."

Knowing the morning at school would arrive too soon, the couple parted and went their separate ways for the night.

♥ ♥ ♥

Opening the door to her home, Ginny heard the mournful whining of a neglected Jezebel. "I'm sorry, Jez. It won't be that much longer and you will see more of me, and hopefully more of your pal, Carlos. I think his master and I will be taking you two on a few more walks after this week."

Once the door opened, Jezebel lifted her nose in the air and trotted out into the yard as she pretended to ignore her owner. Closing the door on her arrogant hound, Ginny opened her tin of doggie treats and chose a snack for the neglected pooch.

When Ginny opened the door to let Jezebel back in, the dog forgot past offenses when she spotted the tasty treat. Slobbery lips reached out to slap across Ginny's hand in gratitude for the morsel of food. Giving the dog a belly rub, her owner yawned and headed for her pajamas.

Falling into bed in total exhaustion, Ginny repeated a memory verse in her mind before thanking God for her day and the success of the musical. Then she and Jezebel curled up together for a short night's sleep.

♥ ♥ ♥

Bleary-eyed from lack of sleep, Ginny greeted her wide-awake students the next morning as the bell rang announcing the start of their day. Thankfully, an afternoon assembly would give Ginny some relief from her responsibilities. Sending her students to the library and physical education classes for two periods of the day provided another blessing. Pasting on her enthusiastic teacher face, she opened class with the usual routines and then asked the children if anyone had anything interesting they would like to share before they turned to their morning math.

Melissa practically bounced out of her seat as she waved her hand excitedly. "Miss Cline, may I share about the musical we're doing? It's really fun everybody, and Miss Cline and I are the stars." Pulling a flash drive from her pocket, she explained that Mrs. Russell took pictures of the rehearsals as a memory for her to keep. "Please, Miss Cline, can you show these on the computer so everyone can see them?"

Ginny bowed to Melissa's plea, and chose to use the pictures as an impromptu lesson on local history. Suddenly finding herself wide-awake and ready to talk about her favorite subject, she turned on the projector for the white board technology found in her classroom. When the pictures appeared on the large screen, she began explaining Forest Glen's involvement in the Underground Railroad while the children watched the slide show.

Melissa beamed with pride as the photos depicted her role in the play. "There I am running across the stage when the slave catcher tried to find us. He can't catch up because Miss Ginny-- oops, I mean Miss Cline is there to show me the hidden room. Oh, and her name isn't Miss Cline in the play, it's Christine Woodson and she's the hero. Is that what you call a girl hero?"

Ginny started to answer but Melissa kept talking.

"Anyway, Christine helps us find a hiding place. Look at the wagon I get to ride in. There's a secret place for my play family to hide in so we can sneak out of town. I have a real nice lady playing my momma in the musical. Her name is Miss Hope. That's a pretty name, isn't it? Did you know Miss Cline wrote the whole play and all the music?"

Ginny could hardly believe the young girl, who had once been so quiet and shy, now spoke without fear and without stopping as she went on about the musical. Pride filled the teacher as she listened to her changed student. The musical not only served as a gift to the community to teach them about the past, it had also served the purpose of bringing a neglected little girl out of her shell.

When pictures of the lead couple came up on the screen, several of the children snickered and one asked if Miss Cline had a boyfriend. Ginny paused and tried to think of a way to explain to the children that she and James were only pretending for the sake of the play.

Melissa spoke up before Ginny could answer. "He's only her boyfriend for the play. She saves her kisses for our director. Mr. Scott's her real boyfriend."

"Oooo, that's mushy stuff."

"Miss Cline has a boyfriend. I'm telling my mom."

Heat suffused Ginny's cheeks and she quickly put an end to the pandemonium that broke out after Melissa's remark. Zipping through the rest of the slides, she hastily turned to the math lesson and managed to keep the children from asking any more personal questions.

❤ ❤ ❤

"James, can you put more support under your singing voice? I feel like you're fading out when you get to the end of a phrase." Scott wondered why the man seemed so out of character.

"I'm trying my best, but I must have eaten something that isn't setting too well with my system." On cue, James grabbed for his abdomen and groaned in pain. "In fact, I may need to sit down for a while."

Taking in James' pasty complexion, Scott suggested that the ailing man call it a night. Hopefully, his condition would not make the rest of the cast sick; especially Ginny. She had the closest contact since they played the leads.

Stepping into the role, Scott welcomed the excuse to hold Ginny's hands and look deeply into her eyes. He didn't have to act when it came to expressing his love for the leading lady and Ginny seemed pleased to fall into her role with someone she really cared about.

The following evening, James called Scott to let him know that whatever bothered him had come and gone several times throughout the day, so he wouldn't come to rehearsal that evening. Promising he would be there for opening night, James thanked him for his understanding. Scott wished the man well and then smiled to himself at the thought of once again getting to play opposite his leading lady. Even the cast seemed delighted with their temporary lead man as they threw themselves into the final dress rehearsal before opening night.

♥ ♥ ♥

When Scott stopped by the men's dressing room on opening night, he noted the heavy amount of makeup covering James' face. "Break a leg everyone." He stepped closer to James and asked, "Are you sure you're feeling well enough to perform?"

"It's nothing I can't handle. Besides, I made a promise to Ginny and this time I'm not going to break it." James winced as he stood and then the two men moved toward the green room where most of the cast had gathered.

"Would you like to join us for a prayer before we go on stage? It's not required, but some of us who are believers feel like it will help make the production better." Ginny's encouraging smile was enough to make anyone want to join the circle gathered in the middle of the room.

"Sure, I think I'm going to need all the prayers I can get," James said.

As the evening progressed, the cast performed with finesse. The audience laughed, cried, and understood the fear of the runaway family, who had several near misses with the slave catcher who followed their trail into the little town of Forest Glen. Cheering their escape and the proposal scene between James and Ginny's characters, the crowd jumped to their feet at the end of the final rousing chorus and curtain call. James and Ginny led the group in their bows as the stage filled with flowers from their adoring fans. Ginny told Scott later that James' hand seemed a little clammy as she held it during the curtain call, but chalked it up to the fact that everyone seemed excited about their success.

♥ ♥ ♥

The second night of their three-night run proved to be just as successful as the first. Another full house guaranteed enough ticket sales to sustain the museum for several years. As the audience leapt to their feet for the evening's final bow, Ginny could see the pain in James' face as they came together from different sides of the stage. Squeezing her hand tightly, James had trouble rising up from their first bow and gave Ginny a look of panic when it was time for another dip. Quickly covering for James, Ginny stepped in front of him and did a deep curtsy that distracted the crowd from the fact that the leading man couldn't bend over.

James moaned in deep pain as the final curtain came down. "I think I may need to make a trip to the emergency room." Looping his arm through Ginny's, he begged for her help as they edged off the stage. "Looks like I'm going to let you down again, Ginny. I'm sorry, but I better get to the hospital before this pain kills me." James doubled over and hugged his abdomen as they stopped and he fell into a nearby chair.

❤ ❤ ❤

Don and Ellen came backstage in time to see Ginny help James to the seat. After a quick assessment of the situation, the Drummonds offered to take James to the emergency room.

Don couldn't help but joke with the man. "Guess you're trying to steal the show by doing a little swan dive here. Maybe they'll have to take me off the drums and do your part for you."

Don did a silly imitation of one of the songs, making James laugh. Unfortunately, the laughter did little for the man's aching gut.

"Oh... Ouch, you're killing me. Get me to your car and instead of driving me crazy, you should drive like crazy."

Don complied and assisted him to the van.

Ginny stared after the vehicle as it pulled from the theater's parking lot. A mix of emotions swirled in her heart as she watched the hero of her musical ride away.

Scott laid a hand on her shoulder. "Don't worry, Ginny. Whatever happens, we've got this."

❤ ❤ ❤

Scott pulled his phone from its charger to answer James' call from the hospital.

"I'm sorry, man. They're prepping me now for the operation or I'd be there to carry on with the show." James moaned and released a deep breath. "I know you'll do okay. After all, you stood in for me a lot lately, since I haven't been feeling the greatest. Besides, you're the director and you've got the whole thing memorized anyway." Medical noises beeped in the background as James groaned out his need to get off the phone.

"We'll be praying for you," Scott reassured the hurting man, as he ended the early morning call. Trying to go back to sleep seemed hopeless so he put on clothes and headed to campus. Letting himself into the empty theater, he turned toward the men's dressing room. The space still smelled of stage makeup and deodorant. A quick look at James' costumes proved the two men were close enough in size that Scott should have no problem donning the leading man's clothing.

He snagged two shirts and a pair of pants used by Joseph's character and stuffed them in a plastic bag someone had left lying on the floor. It wouldn't hurt to send those items through his washing machine and dryer. For some reason, washing away the lingering scent of James' aftershave gave him a sense of pleasure.

After he finished looking over the costumes, Scott decided to make a quick check of the props required for the leading man role. As he stared at the locket that would be given to his leading lady in the proposal scene, his mind began to calculate a completely different approach to the scene; an approach that would become very real to both his beloved Ginny and to himself. Pocketing the locket and the ribbon that held it, Scott whistled as he headed home to get ready for the rest of his busy day.

♥ ♥ ♥

"You're a woman after God's own heart, my sweet lady. I don't know of anyone as brave or as strong in spirit as you are. Every day I learn something new about you and each revelation makes me love you more and more. Will you do me the honor of becoming my bride?"

As Ginny looked into her suitor's eyes, she could hardly believe Scott only played a role. His deep blue eyes seemed to reach into her very being as he knelt before her to ask for her hand in marriage. Something shifted in her chest when he finished stating the proposal.

"I mean it, Ginny."

She barely heard his quiet whisper as he rose on cue to hug her close after her scripted answer. Reaching into his pocket, he began the lines about the family locket as he drew out the velvet ribbon that normally held the locket at the end of its length. Sliding the ribbon over his hand until it reached its loop, Scott raised it to reveal a glittering antique emerald cut diamond ring dangling in place of the usual pendant. He began to say his line, only differently.

"Dear lady, will you accept my ring and my heart for the rest of our lives? Together we will work for freedom as we build each other up in love."

Ginny stared at the ring for only a second before her eyes moved to make loving contact with Scott's. Throwing her arms around him she whispered, so that only he could hear, "Yes, Scott."

Taking the ring from the ribbon, Scott slid it on Ginny's finger with a flourish and reached out to embrace her again. Their unscripted kiss brought a rousing applause from the audience as Ginny gathered her wits and continued with the lines she had written for the leading lady, never dreaming the words would be real lines of acceptance to the leading man in her personal life.

"Yes, I will accept your love for the rest of our lives. Together we'll bring freedom to travelers who come to us seeking help. We will grow in our love for each other and in service to those in need."

Gazing into her eyes, Scott smiled as he continued the scripted lines. "I'll always be there for you. You'll never have to be alone in your efforts, my love. As your husband, I'll be able to see to your desires and their needs at all times as we join our lives in a love that will endure forever."

Scott couldn't resist sneaking in another unscripted kiss, to the delight of Ginny and the audience.

"Enough kissing already!" Derrick added his own break from the script. "Let's get this show on the road. We've got to get these runaways out of town so we can have our big celebration." After a brief round of laughter, the cast pulled their act together and finished the final rendition of *Incident at Woodson House*. The cheering audience's standing ovation grew to a deafening roar. Ginny and Scott took their places on the stage for their final bows with the ensemble and snuck in a final kiss after they announced to everyone that a real proposal had just taken place.

Epilogue

Jessie and Annie fussed over Ginny's white velvet gown and flowing veil as they waited for their cue from the wedding organizer. Her mother's handmade lace veil provided the perfect addition for Ginny's Christmas ensemble. The tiny hearts, roses, and dogs woven along the veil's edge spoke of her mother's unique style, but were subtle enough to satisfy the bride's modest taste. The white cloud of lace would be something Ginny would cherish and hopefully hand down to a daughter some time in the distant future. A delicate heart-shaped blue sapphire necklace from Roy provided the perfect "something blue." The pillow holding the rings from Scott's grandparents, and now their own, filled the role of something old and borrowed just for the wedding.

Peeping out the window of the mansion's powder room, Ginny observed the white gazebo in the historical village's garden bedecked in white ribbons and gauzy puffs of tulle. Christmas lights and wreaths decorated the gates that led to the garden. Guests snuggled together on chairs covered in white velour as gentle snowflakes fell, creating the perfect backdrop for a Christmas wedding.

She found it hard to believe it had been just over half a year since she stood in this very building, shaking in her boots, prepared to present her pitch for her musical to the influential group of dignitaries and an unknown professor of theater. Today the only boots she stood in were a lovely pair of white heeled ones tucked neatly under her wedding dress. The only trembling going on today came from extreme happiness.

Because of that event many months ago, her dream of creating and presenting the musical had become a reality that she would remember for the rest of her life. No longer quaking in fear of the unknown, Ginny bravely stood ready to begin her next step of fulfilling another dream; the dream of marrying the man she had grown to love and trust during a glorious fall filled with the bright colors of a changing season full of love.

Many long walks with their dogs and evenings spent together as they graded papers from their respective teaching positions had only caused their love to grow deeper. Together they decided that Ginny's little house would be a good source of rental income and after today she would move into the house of her dreams that Scott had lived in since the day he moved to Forest Glen. At this moment, Jezebel and Carlos lounged in the laundry room of Scott's historical home where they would spend the following week with Ginny's brother Nathan, who would be house- and dog-sitting.

A knock on the door let the ladies know the time had come for the mother of the bride to take her place. Slipping a warm white cape over her daughter's wedding dress, Jessie gave her another hug and turned her over to Roy, who patiently waited in the hallway of the old mansion. His wedding outfit resembled something from a Currier and Ives Christmas scene with his warm coat and colorful mom-made scarf capped off with a jaunty top hat.

Her maids of honor, Kara and Melody led the bridal procession. Melody's newly adopted twins walked near the bridesmaids as ring bearer and flower girl. Annie, the matron of honor, dressed in a long woolen skirt with a matching green cape, made her way into the gazebo garden, setting the stage for the bride's entrance. Ginny, on Roy's arm, took her place at the garden gate and then they made their way to where the minister, with Scott's brother Robert, her brother Nathan, and a forgiven James stood as groomsmen. Scott stood at the center of the gazebo. His yearning look of love as they approached sent tingles through Ginny's heart.

Roy whispered a sweet message to Ginny before he placed her hands into Scott's welcoming palms. "If your mother accepts my proposal, I hope to be your real father one day. I pray your life with Scott will be filled with God's love." His sweet kiss on her cheek made Ginny smile.

Then the ceremony of their dreams began right on cue. Hope's warm voice sang a song of love and dedication, which the loving couple had composed together. Ellen played a delicate accompaniment for Hope's song as she stretched over her expanded belly to reach the portable piano keyboard. Honey and her band played a soft rendition of the proposal song from the musical when they exchanged rings. Scott and Ginny smiled their thanks to the musicians sheltered in their tent, before returning to gaze at each other with adoration as they spoke vows of love and commitment.

Ginny looked up into Scott's eyes, as the minister pronounced his final declaration of their married state, and saw both of their dreams of love completed in his heart-filled gaze.

He wrapped his warm arms around Ginny and they kissed for the first thrilling moment as a married couple. "I love you, Mrs. Hallmark."

"I love you too, Dr. Hallmark...more than you'll ever know."

"We've got a lifetime for you to teach me about your love, sweetheart." Scott gently placed his wife's arm through his and they walked down the garden path, accepting congratulations from their adoring friends, as they stepped toward their new life together.

ABOUT THE AUTHOR

Bettie Boswell is an author, illustrator, and composer for both Christian and children's markets. From high school onward, she has loved creating words and music to enrich the lives of others. It all started with skits for her church youth group, which led to involvement in Christian camp skits and worship songs. As a minister's wife she shares her talents with her church as pianist and choir director. When she isn't writing, drawing or composing, she keeps busy with her day job, teaching at the elementary level in northwest Ohio

Her numerous musicals have been performed at schools, churches, and two community theater events. Her involvement with community musicals inspired her to write *On Cue.*

Like Ginny and Scott, she and her husband have had basset hounds and Chihuahuas for pets. Currently, they are owned by one tuxedo cat. They enjoy spending time with their two grown sons, a daughter-in-law, and three grandchildren.

Find her on the Internet:

https://sites.google.com/view/bettieboswellauthorillustrator/home

https://twitter.com/BboswellB

https://www.facebook.com/bettie.boswell.9

CPSIA information can be obtained
at www.ICGtesting.com
Printed in the USA
FSHW021646041120
75440FS